ELF & OWL DOG & HEAD

ELF & OWL
DOG & HEAD

ELF & OWL DOG & HEAD

M. T. ANDERSON

illustrated by JUNYI WU

CANDLEWICK PRESS

Text copyright © 2023 by M. T. Anderson
Illustrations copyright © 2023 by Junyi Wu

First edition 2023

Library of Congress Catalog Card Number 2022936763
ISBN 978-1-5362-2281-4

23 24 25 26 27 28 APS 10 9 8 7 6 5 4 3 2 1

Printed in Humen, Dongguan, China

This book was typeset in Adobe Caslon Pro.
The illustrations were done in pencil.

Candlewick Press
99 Dover Street
Somerville, Massachusetts 02144

www.candlewick.com

A JUNIOR LIBRARY GUILD SELECTION

To LaRue,

who escaped from the Kingdom Under the Mountain

MTA

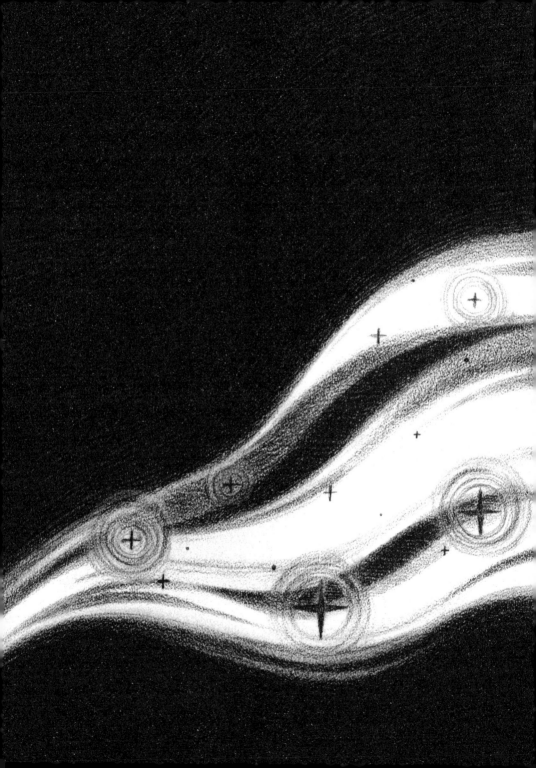

Chapter One

It was Monday, so they were hunting wyrms in the petrified forest. That's what the Queen Under the Mountain always scheduled for Monday. The pack of elf-hounds bounded past stone trees, barking and howling. They poured through the wood like a tide. Behind them rode dukes and duchesses, lords and ladies, servants and sorcerers. Huntsmen blew huge, curling horns.

They chased a wyrm that was old and clever. She slithered over boulders and under fallen trees of metal, glancing back to see if she had lost the elf-hounds yet. Several times, they paused to catch the scent of her again. They sniffed the cavern air. Then one of the dogs spotted the flick of the wyrm's tail, barked warning, and plunged after the monster. The whole pack followed.

The whole pack except for one. She was a young elf-hound, slim and elegant, with bright, sharp eyes. She held back. She watched the other dogs surge forward. Her eye was caught by movement far off to the side, up a hill of marble oak trees with spreading branches. She had seen the wyrm's children, squiggly baby wyrms: the mother was leading the dog pack away from them on purpose so her children could escape. The elf-hound watched the infant wyrms flee unnoticed.

The lords and ladies rode up behind the elf-hound. They would reward her if she led the whole Royal Hunt to the fleeing young.

"What's wrong with this one?" asked one of the knights. "She's just standing there."

"She'd be one of our best dogs," said the Master of the Hunt, "if she wasn't always dreaming of something else."

"Well," said a duke, "force her to get moving! She should join the rest of the pack!"

"Go, girl!" yelled the Master of the Hunt, and he kicked out at her with his boot to let her know who was boss.

The elegant elf-hound stared at him coldly. He didn't deserve to know what she'd seen. Almost smiling, she started after the pack again, barking as loudly as she could, as if she'd never noticed the young wyrm efts scrambling to safety up the hill. As if she'd never figured out the old wyrm's plan, leading the Hunt away from the precious young.

She reached the pack, hopping over huge mushrooms and shelves of fungus. Easily, she soared past stragglers.

The People Under the Mountain kept the petrified forest stocked with wyrms and basilisks and other hungry beasts, just so they could hunt them without having to risk going aboveground. Outside the caves, above the mountain, the woods were deeper and wider, but sometimes haunted by humans.

Usually, the elf-hounds only got to hunt in these two square miles of cavern, seeking out monsters that had been bred by their masters for sport. But the old blue wyrm was leading the pack out of the familiar tunnels and caves. The dogs could tell. She was leading them upward.

"Smart old cow," said one of the dukes. "Should we let her get out of the caves? Shall we follow her? Or shall I order the gates slammed shut? What do we think?"

"Good day for a hunt," said a count, squinting after the wyrm through his rune-covered monocle. "Let's go aboveground. Hunt her up there. It'll be good for the elf-hounds to have a change of scene. We have the wizards with us. They can hide us from the humans."

And so, with great horns blaring behind them, the pack tumbled up the passage that led out of the petrified forest, out of the caverns, and into the bright sunlight of the forest aboveground.

The old wyrm flung herself along, delighted. She had saved her children. And she herself might escape into this new, bright world. She just had to lead the dogs a little farther. Then she'd give them the slip.

Outside, it was spring, and the woods were just starting to turn green. The sky was a brilliant blue, and the sun picked out the red riding jackets of the knights and lords and ladies and the gems on their swords and tridents.

Their wizards rode to either side of the Hunt, cranking magical machines that sputtered out smoke. The People Under the Mountain only lived half in the world of humans, as if they had stepped with one leg into another time or an unseen place. This smoke would make them completely invisible if they stumbled across any humans lost in the woods.

The dog pack was wild with excitement. They rarely got to visit the world outside the palaces and parks in the caverns under the mountain. Some of them were afraid of the light. Some of them were worried that there were no walls of rock to protect them. They just bounded forward and tried to focus on the retreating wyrm.

But the young dog with the sharp eyes was fascinated by everything she saw and wanted to see more. She was trained to explore forests and learn their secret ways. She wanted to investigate this sparkling woodland that lay on the top side of the mountain, where she saw colors she had never seen before.

Greykin, the young dog's uncle, was close on the wyrm's tail. He was a prize elf-hound, a leader of the pack. The wyrm reared up and slashed at him. He ducked back.

The dogs were all around the wyrm then. They did not know that she was trying to protect her young. They only knew that they had been trained to kill beasts like her for the amusement of their masters. They barked furiously.

Except the young and elegant elf-hound, who had spotted something she had never seen before. It was the back of a gas station. It was made of cement blocks. The woods went right up to it.

Her uncle Greykin caught her eye. What was she doing? She should start barking, screaming—she should prepare to leap and tear at the scaly monster.

The wyrm was cornered. Behind her was a road. A highway. Humans drove past in cars, unaware that a few inches from their windows, a great and bloody battle was about to begin.

The dogs closed in. It looked like several of them were about to die in the fight. The People Under the Mountain did not care. They had plenty of dogs.

Growling, the pack closed in, step by step. The wyrm swung her front claws. She snapped at them.

The dogs' muscles twitched. They were ready to leap.

The huntsman blew the horn—the signal for the kill.

And the wyrm threw herself backward and hurtled across the road, swaying her long blue body to eel between speeding cars.

The dogs just stood there, astonished, their mouths open. A few still remembered to bark.

They saw the wyrm jump up on top of a van with a loud thump. Then they saw her leap off the other side, into the safety of the woods there.

The van swerved: the driver must have heard the thump and maybe even caught a glimpse, out of the corner of their eye, of flashing blue scales. There was a lot of honking.

The dukes and duchesses and knights and ladies all were angry. They had wanted to see a spectacular fight. Now the

wyrm had escaped, and the dogs couldn't reach her over the tide of humans in their vehicles.

The hunt was over. The duke made a sign to the huntsman, who blew a retreat on his horn. The People Under the Mountain turned their horses around slowly and headed back toward the entrance to the cave, muttering angrily.

The dogs still barked at the wyrm across the busy highway. A Chihuahua in a truck barked back, furious. But no one else could hear them.

The hunting horns blew again. From the highway, the car horns honked. The dogs knew it was time to go home. One by one, they turned tail and trotted toward their masters.

The mystical fog drifted through the trees, growing fainter. Soon, the spring breeze blew it away completely. It was as if the hunt had never happened.

Except there was one dog left behind. The young, elegant elf-hound with the sharp eye. She was standing in the middle of the gas station parking lot, inspecting cars. She had never seen cars before. They smelled strange. She had never smelled plastic before, and she'd only smelled gasoline when the Queen Under the Mountain went up in her flying machine. The door to the gas station opened with a jingle. The most incredible smells wafted out. The elf-hound was used to being served food in a golden bowl in her kennel far beneath the earth. But she had never smelled pizza before. This, surely, was a food so royal that the Queen herself had never dined upon it.

"Look at the dog," said a little girl. "She's pretty."

"Wonder where her owner is," said a father, looking around the parking lot.

At this, the elf-hound realized that she had fallen far behind her pack. She looked around, startled. She had planned to catch up with them. Time to run.

She sprinted away from the gas station and the highway and back into the forest. She ran through spruce woods and pine woods and a stand of maples. She ran to the bottom of the mountain.

It was almost night when she got there. She sniffed at the ground, following the scent of her brothers and sisters. She smelled the horses of the Royal Hunt. Their track led right up to a huge cliff face.

Then it stopped.

But wasn't that where they had come out? Hadn't they all tumbled out into the sunlight in exactly this spot?

But now time and magic and the curtain between worlds had shifted, and the door was not there anymore.

The dog huffed deep in her throat—irritated to be left behind. She walked back and forth through the underbrush, sniffing.

They were gone. All of her pack. Her brothers and sisters. Her parents and aunts and her uncle Greykin. They were all gone, deep under the mountain, and she had no way to follow them.

She pawed at the blank stone. Her claws scratched across the granite.

Deep in her throat, for the first time in her life, she whimpered.

But no one would come for her.

She was all alone, trapped in the world aboveground.

Chapter Two

There is no dumber game to play alone than Frisbee.

That is what Clay was thinking as he was walking through the forest with a Frisbee. He was alone.

There was a virus all across the country and the world. Pretty much everything had shut down. Even school was closed. None of his friends were allowed to come over. He could play with his sisters, but he would rather die in a pit than do that. His little sister, Juniper, was a know-it-all, and his big sister, DiRossi, spent all of her time playing war games online, hogging the computer.

Clay hadn't seen his best friend, Levi, for a couple of months. He didn't have anyone to kick around a ball with, or build stuff with, or throw a Frisbee with.

As he walked along through the forest, he tried a game where he threw the Frisbee straight up. Maybe he could perfect the flick of a wrist so when he saw Levi again, he would be a Frisbee master. The Frisbee sliced upward above the tops of the pines. It spun there for a second in the sun, wobbled, and then fell helter-skelter back down toward the ground. Clay ran to grab it out of the air.

It clunked him on the head. Then it flopped over onto the moss.

Clay bent to pick it up. He was kind of glad no one saw. It was better to practice being a Frisbee master alone.

Except it felt like someone had seen.

Clay looked around the clearing. He felt watched.

He did not notice, behind him, the glint of blue scales. He did not hear the six crooked claws pacing toward him across the moss. But somehow, he felt the glare of the large golden eyes on his back.

Half bent over, the Frisbee in his hand, Clay inspected the dark woods in front of him. There were deep shadows under the firs and spruce. He took a careful step backward.

Though he did not know it, something behind him was taking careful steps forward and opening its toothy mouth.

Clay backed up slowly, right toward that mouth.

The golden eyes behind him slowly blinked, and the creature's smile widened.

Clay saw something burst out of the woods in front of him—a violent blur of white—something darting forward, barking crazily.

A dog! A mad dog! It was sprinting right toward him, growling and baying.

It must have rabies! he thought. *It's going to bite me!*

He looked around for something on the ground—a branch or a rock—to protect himself. Nothing!

Stupidly, he held up the only thing he had with him—the Frisbee—as if it were a knight's shield. He waited for the dog to strike.

But the dog ran right past him.

He swiveled around. Something was scrambling into the woods. The dog was chasing it, barking warnings.

From the crashing in the blackberry bushes, it sounded like it must be something pretty big.

The slim white dog stood at the edge of the clearing, legs stiff, tail straight up, ears out, and issued barks like threats and commands.

It must have been a bear behind him, Clay figured. There were black bears in this forest. They didn't usually bother people.

They were scared of people. But maybe this bear hadn't been a normal bear, but a bear with an evil turn of mind.

That must be it. This dog had just saved him from a bear with an evil turn of mind.

"Thanks, dog," Clay said.

She turned to look at him. She didn't want to take her eyes off the forest for long. With a piercing gaze, she studied the shadows. A few spruce boughs wriggled as something big climbed under them.

Clay had never seen a dog like her. She was thin like a greyhound or a whippet. She was milk white. She had tall, pointed ears. And the inside of those ears was red. That was the strangest thing. The red pointed ears.

She was someone's dog. She had a collar on. It was an ugly collar, too glitzy, with lots of fake pearls and diamonds and rubies.

"Is the bear still around?" Clay asked the dog, walking over to her side. "You going to protect me, huh?" He knew it was polite to talk to dogs like they can talk back.

The dog quivered with watchfulness.

"You're a good . . ." He leaned down and checked. "A good girl."

She turned and looked into his eyes and blinked once. As if to say: *Of course I am.*

That was how Clay met the elf-hound.

For a long time, she watched the woods. And then she sniffed the air, her black nose flexing, trying to find a scent of the beast that had passed.

"Do you know how to play Frisbee?" Clay asked the dog. He twitched the Frisbee as if he were about to throw it. He wanted to see if she knew the game, if she ran in anticipation. She just stared at him.

So he tried shouting, "Fetch!" and threw the Frisbee. It soared across the clearing, hit a pine, and thudded to the dirt. The dog watched it all with mild interest.

"No," said Clay. "You're supposed to go get it. Fetch. Fetch!"

She looked at him like a queen trying to decipher a foreign language.

He trudged over and picked up the Frisbee. "Stupid dog," he muttered.

He threw the Frisbee over her head. It was a good throw. She peacefully watched it swish right by her and land in a blackberry bush.

Clay rolled his eyes. That blackberry bush was going to be a pain to crawl through. He shook his head and groaned.

And then he blinked, because the dog was right at his side with the Frisbee in her mouth. He had not seen her move. She was sitting daintily on the moss, presenting the Frisbee to him like a gift.

He took it from her mouth. How had she done that? It was like she had run invisibly.

Clay threw the Frisbee again, to see if she would repeat the trick.

The elf-hound was a little confused by this human child. She knew he was not one of the People Under the Mountain: he looked like them, but his ears weren't at all pointed. He seemed like a nice person, but he could not keep hold of his odd little shield. Did he really expect her to keep picking it up if he was going to drop it all over the forest and hurl it into treetops? She supposed it was worth the trouble—it was made of some precious substance, subtle in color as jade but tough as bone and light as paper, smelling of this new human world and its miracles.

They played Frisbee for a while. Several times, the same odd thing happened: when Clay threw the Frisbee into some-place hard to reach, he would not see the dog fetch it, but she would appear right next to him, laying it at his feet.

So he deliberately threw it into a treetop. It swayed in a

pine branch, then dropped down, skittering from branch to branch, and came to rest about ten feet from the ground.

Clay watched the dog carefully. He wanted to see when she disappeared.

She sat on her haunches and watched him back.

"Okay, do your trick," he said to her. She stared at him without blinking.

"Fetch with magic!" he said.

She wagged her tail slightly, but not much.

They had a staring contest for several minutes. Then he went to climb the tree and get the Frisbee out of it. He was pulling himself up from branch to branch when the dog gave a quick, sharp bark from down below.

"One sec," said Clay, straining to reach up. He fumbled in the pine needles, trying to feel the rim of the Frisbee.

She barked again. He looked down. She had the Frisbee sitting in front of her.

"You are a really good dog," he said.

She looked at him as if to say, *Yes. We both already know that.*

When it came time for him to go home, he said goodbye and set off on the path that led back through the woods. The dog trotted after him.

"Your owner is going to be mad," he told her. "Go home. Go home!"

She looked at him with surprise. She seemed a little hurt.

"Go home!" he ordered, and flicked his fingers in the air. She sat still.

"I'm sorry, girl," he said, and went to scratch her head. She bowed away from his fingers. She did not want to be touched by a stranger.

"See you again sometime," he said. "Thanks for the bear."

He left her sitting on the path. He went down through the forest. All around him were plastic lines strung from tree to tree where his neighbors the Lupiceks did their maple sugaring.

Then, there was the dog in front of him on the path, heading right for him. Somehow, she had passed him without him even seeing. When she saw him, she stopped, checked his face to see that he approved, and then she darted off on the path ahead of him.

"You're a scout dog," said Clay. He was impressed.

When they came to a fork in the path, she waited for him to tell her which way to go. He pointed toward his house, and she ran in that direction, leaping over tree trunks.

As Clay got close to home, he started to slow down. He wasn't too eager to get back. The whole family had been stuck in the house together for months because of the disease. His dad left to go to work—he was the village's road commissioner, so he had to plow snow and flatten the dirt roads and stop the mud roads from crumbling into the rivers during rain. Clay's mom was a waitress at the Gerenford Diner, and she had lost her job because the diner had closed—there were no customers anymore, with the sickness. So most days, Clay sat with his sisters and his mom, and she made them all do schoolwork. They had to share the computer between the three of them, which was nearly impossible, because his little sister, Juniper, always wanted to watch stupid cartoons with round-head people shaking hands and waving, and his older sister, DiRossi, had to do about a thousand hours of homework on the computer, and then she wanted to play zombie games with her friends. There was never time for Clay to do what he needed to do or to talk with his friends.

And his sisters didn't stop bugging him even at night. Clay shared a room with Juniper and all her stuffed animals. She wanted everything kept neat and clean and in order. Even though she was two years younger than him, she was always giving him lectures about how he was messy and needed to clean up. He wasn't messy; he just wanted the stuff in his room to be where he left it. That seemed fair to him.

Since the start of the virus, Clay and his sisters could pretty much not stand each other.

He rambled down the hill to the house. The dog was already poking around, exploring, sniffing at the shed.

"All right," said Clay to the dog. "I've got to go in to do school stuff. Bye!"

He went into the house.

His mother asked, "How was the woods?"

"Stupid," said Clay. "I can't see any friends, and I was attacked by a bear."

His mom was surprised. "Attacked by a bear? Really?"

"Yeah. That dog saved me." He pointed out the window.

"Ooh," said Juniper. "She's pretty."

"Don't look at her," said Clay. "I'm the one who found her."

His mom was very serious, though. "Clay, if you were attacked by a bear, we need to call Fish and Wildlife and let them know."

"Why?" said Juniper. "The wildlife obviously know already."

"The *Department* of Fish and Wildlife," said their mom.

Clay crossed his arms. Juniper was the only person who could be a know-it-all and still at the same time know nothing.

"Was it a bear?" his mom demanded.

He said, "It was bear-like."

"An *actual bear*, Clay?"

"Yeah. The dog chased it away."

She took out her phone.

"Or," said Clay, "it could have been a deer. I didn't get a good look at it."

Juniper sneered, "You can't tell the difference between a deer and a bear?"

"Naw," said Clay. "I also can't tell the difference between a sister and a jerk."

"Clay!" his mother scolded. "Apologize!"

They worked on school stuff through the afternoon.

The dog didn't leave Clay's yard. She sat patiently outside the door, facing outward, as if guarding them from danger.

Clay's father got home in the town's orange truck. The dog barked at him as he walked toward the house until Clay stuck his head out and said to her, "It's okay. That's my dad."

The whole family was interested in the dog.

"She's a beautiful dog," said Clay's father.

"Those red ears are weird," said DiRossi. Ever since the sickness had shut everything down, DiRossi had been grumpy. She spent most of her time blowing things up on the computer or sleeping in her room or making up tragic things to say. "Maybe it means she has rabies. She'll probably eat you in your sleep."

Clay's mother gave DiRossi a Look and then said, "We should see if anyone's missing a dog. We can call the town constable and check on the town forum."

Juniper said, "What kind of a breed is she? I want to look it up. Mom, can we look it up?"

Juniper always had to know the name for everything and how everything fit into its place. It drove Clay crazy. He'd found this dog.

"It doesn't matter what breed she is," he said.

"I've never seen a dog like her before," said DiRossi.

"Yes, let's look it up!" said their mother.

"On the computer," said Juniper, snuggling into her mother's lap.

"We look for 'dog breeds' and 'red ears,'" said her mother.

Clay suddenly wanted to punch Juniper. "The dog's not a breed!" he said. It was like Juniper was stealing his dog by finding a thing to call it.

"Just because you don't know the kind of breed doesn't mean she isn't one," said Juniper.

Clay said, "I know what breed she is. I know. She's a magical dog."

Juniper pointed to dogs on the screen. "She looks kind of like that. And like that."

"That's a whippet," her mother said. "And that's a dingo."

This was all Clay could take. His dog was not a dingo. He yelled at his sister, "I said I know her breed! She's a . . ." He thought for a second. "She's a *Bulgarian elf-hound*, okay?"

He didn't know where the phrase "elf-hound" had come from. It just made sense because of her pointed ears. He also didn't know where Bulgaria was, but it seemed far enough away that no one in his family would know whether they had elf-hounds there.

In the silence after he yelled, his father looked at him in confusion. "You okay, kid?" he said.

"She's my dog," Clay said. "She saved me from a bear. I know what breed she is."

"She's not your dog," said Clay's mother. "And we should put a note on the village *Fireside Forum* to see who's missing her. Obviously someone loves her."

They scanned through the *Fireside Forum* listings for the last several days. No one in town had reported a dog missing. Clay's mother put a note on the forum saying, "DOG FOUND: White. Remarkable ears. Contact the O'Brians."

Clay's mother got out a tin food dish from when they'd had a cat and put some sardines in it. She had Clay put it out on the porch for the dog.

The elf dog sniffed at the dish but wouldn't eat. Though the O'Brians did not know it, she was used to eating off of plates of silver and gold. She could not believe she was being offered food on tin. But on the other hand, she hadn't eaten for more than a day.

Clay reported, "It looks like she wants to eat, but she's not eating."

The dog, waiting for a better dish, gave the human child a look that she believed would convey *I am a royal elf-hound of the People Under the Mountain, and I am used to being served by page boys with platters.*

Clay looked into her eyes. "What's wrong, girl?" he asked.

She reached out a paw and very delicately pushed the dish away.

"I think she's afraid of the tin dish," said Clay. "It rattled loud when I put it down."

Clay's mother, tight-mouthed, came to the door with a plastic dish. She reached out past Clay, picked up the tin dish with its sardines, and dumped them into the plastic dish. She plopped the plastic down. "Okay?" she said to Clay. "Better?"

The elf-hound looked at the dainty little fishes, served upon a dish made of that remarkable metal like bone—red, this time, the deep red of a dragon's tongue or her own noble ears.

This—*this* was how you treated a royal elf-hound of the People Under the Mountain. These people were taking good care of her.

She slurped up the fish in an instant. She was very hungry.

That evening, no one called the O'Brians or wrote to them looking for the dog.

"Can she sleep up in my room?" Clay begged.

"*Our* room," said Juniper.

The elf-hound watched the people argue over where she should sleep. She had slept the night before on the cold, hard ground. She did not mind that. Sleeping on the dirt was good and simple. But normally she slept in the royal kennels on cushions of satin, and in the morning, the page boys would come with special rollers to clean the pillows of fur. Far above, in the stone arches, the royal hunting bats shuffled in and out all night, wearing their little scarlet coats and tiny metal helmets. As she watched the family argue, the dog started to suspect that they did not have a royal kennel. Maybe not even a flock of hunting bats.

"Upstairs," said Clay. "Come upstairs with me."

"And with me," said Juniper. "Come on, doggy."

"Juniper!" growled Clay.

Curious, the dog followed them up the stairs. She walked

into their room and peered around. She smelled the rug and Clay's clothes on the floor.

Clay hoped the dog would decide to jump up on his bed and curl up beside him. But she was somehow too proud and queenly for him even to suggest it. It had to be her decision. He waited patiently for her to explore the room.

Juniper said, "Come on up on my bed, doggo!"

Clay was furious. Didn't Juniper understand?

Juniper jumped up and down on her bed. "Come on, dog!"

"She'll sleep where she wants!" said Clay.

But it broke his heart to think the dog might choose his sister.

Anxious, he watched the dog stand proudly on their rug, looking from one bed to another. It seemed almost as if she was used to something fancier. She was a magic dog—maybe she was used to a big mansion? Clay felt like he might disappoint her.

But the elf-hound could not believe her luck. Truly, these humans understood her importance. They did not put her in a stone kennel with other dogs. No, for the first time in her life, she was allowed to *sleep near people*. To sleep with the pack of persons!

She walked to the end of Clay's bed and curled up on the floor there on an old sweatshirt.

Clay could not stop looking at her as he fell asleep. A magic dog. Who knew what adventures they would have together tomorrow?

Her ribs rose and fell as she slept.

CHAPTER THREE

The elf-hound dreamed of chasing the tentacled shuglume and the wicked grue through caverns under the mountain. She dreamed of coursing along with the dog pack while the horns and bugles of the Hunt blew far behind her, echoing through caves lit by glowing gemstones.

When she woke up, she was shocked for a minute to find herself in a place she didn't know. Immediately, she missed her brothers and sisters and uncles and cousins. They should be sleeping curled all around her. The older dogs should be walking among them already, touching noses, preparing them for the day's hunt. It was strange to be alone. The elf-hound only knew what to do when she was with the pack, all the dogs who had known her since birth. Alone, she didn't know exactly who to be or how to act her part.

The boy was still sleeping. The little girl was making her bed. That was what had woken the elf-hound up. Juniper was tucking in the sheets and humming to herself.

There was something chewing through the wall. The elf-hound could hear it ticking in rhythm. She went over to smell it. The wall was hot. She started barking at it. Whatever was hiding in the wall, it was her job to frighten it away!

"Shhh!" said Juniper, and Clay opened his eyes and sat straight up in his bed.

He said, "What is it, girl?"

He crawled over to see what she was so excited about.

She was barking at the electric heat. It had just turned on and was making a ticking sound.

"It's okay, girl. That's just the heater," said Clay.

She wasn't used to walls making sounds on their own.

It was even worse when Clay went down to breakfast with the dog at his heels. His dad was leaving for work and turned on the dishwasher. The roar startled the dog, and she skittered across the room, barking wildly, unsure whether to protect Clay or shelter behind him.

"Quiet! Quiet!" yelled Clay's mother.

"She's scared!" said Clay. "She doesn't know what's going on!"

"Yeah," said Juniper, for once being useful. "She's scared."

The dog wanted to be brave, but the growling and sloshing of the machine was unlike anything she had ever heard. She was grateful that the boy and the little girl seemed so calm and sure of themselves.

Juniper reached out to pet the dog and reassure her. The dog wriggled away and went to stand just outside the kitchen, keeping an eye on the dishwasher in case it reached out a giant metallic hand and grabbed someone to eat.

"It's like she's never seen a dishwasher before," whispered Juniper.

"Yeah," said Clay. "I wonder what the people who own her are like."

That morning, it was Clay's turn to use the computer. Juniper didn't need it, and DiRossi was still asleep. These days, DiRossi tried to sleep as late as possible, hibernating in her dark cave.

Clay called his best friend, Levi.

"Levi," he said, "I found a dog."

"Can I see her?"

Clay swiveled the computer so Levi could see.

"She's cool-looking," said Levi. "What breed is she?"

"Bulgarian elf-hound," said Clay knowledgeably.

"Can you keep her?"

"Naw. She belongs to someone else." Clay leaned close to the laptop and whispered, "Levi, I think she's magical. She can kind of jump a little from place to place invisibly."

"You sure?"

"Yeah. I'm pretty sure."

"Ohhh!" Levi groaned. "I wish I could come over so we could run tests!"

"I know!"

"Where did you find her?" Levi asked.

"Out in the woods. A little ways up Mount Norumbega."

Levi nodded. "Figures," he said. "My grandpa says that there are a lot of weird things living up in those woods."

"Your grandpa says all sorts of things."

"He's right! It's true!" Levi protested. "People have seen all kinds of things out there. You know. Lights floating up at the top of the mountain. Strange animals. People dressed up like long ago. And you know why? You know what the secret is?" He leaned close to the screen, his voice a whisper.

Clay was intrigued. He asked, "Why?"

"Three words."

"What?"

"U-F-O."

"That's one word."

"It's three words made into one. Unidentified Flying Objects."

Clay sat back in his chair and rolled his eyes. "It is not UFOs."

"She's an alien dog."

"She's not alien!"

"Her mother is a golden retriever, and her father is from another planet. She's an experiment."

Clay wanted to say that was ridiculous, but when he thought about how she had seemed to flicker around the woods, reappearing, it didn't seem so crazy.

"I'm going to take her out for a walk today," said Clay.

"Ohhhhhh," groaned Levi again. "I'm so jealous. I wish I could come along!"

"I know!"

"I know!"

"I know you know!"

It was so frustrating to only see your friends on a screen.

After Clay's school stuff was done, he told his mom he wanted to walk the dog in the woods and see if she recognized the way back home. His mom was inspecting the garden, looking at all the plants that hadn't made it through the winter, and she wasn't paying much attention. "That's a good idea," said Clay's mother. "Maybe she can lead you to her house, and you can find her owner."

Clay hadn't meant the dog's home. He'd meant his own—he wanted to see whether she could find her way back to his house from the middle of the woods. Secretly, he was already hoping that nobody would call the family to claim the dog, and that she had forgotten which direction she had originally come from. He didn't want her old owner to miss her and be sad, but on the other hand, he really wanted her to stay with him.

"Time to start working with the garden," said his mother, shaking her head. She carefully lifted a strand of one of the rosebushes, avoiding the thorns, and let it drop. "It's getting warmer," she said. "The winter left everything a big mess out here. And this summer, we're really going to need the vegetables. I don't know what's going on with my job at the diner. It looks like I'm going to be out of work for a while. We need to save on groceries." She squatted down to prod the dirt in the raised vegetable beds. "And it worries me to go to the grocery store, because of the virus. I want to go as little as possible."

Clay suggested, "You wouldn't have to go to the store as often if you just bought a bunch of party-size bags of ranch-and-onion chips."

His mother gave him a look. "Have fun in the woods," she said. "Don't get lost."

"I'm sorry you're worried about food and all," said Clay.

"Thanks, honey," said his mother. "Really, have a good time. It's not your problem."

He and the dog ran into the forest.

They rambled around for an hour or so on the paths that Clay knew: old logging trails or paths used by people maple sugaring. The dog always ran about twenty or thirty feet ahead of him, poking her snout into stone walls, scanning the trees, and sniffing the air.

At each branch of the path, she'd stop and look back at him, waiting for him to point which way they should go.

Clay decided he would stop giving her instructions. He would just follow her. He wanted to see where she went.

They came to a fork in the path, and he wouldn't point either way.

The elf-hound waited. She was confused. Could he really want her to lead the way without instructions? Where would she go without a command? Without a beast to chase or a huntsman yelling behind her?

"Go where you want to go," said Clay. "I'm just going to follow."

The dog didn't know exactly what to do. But she had noticed that the boy never seemed to follow the magical paths or the tracks that led through time. He never seemed to notice the scent of beasts from other worlds skulking through the woods a few weeks before. It was almost like he couldn't see any of that. So she decided to lead him on one of the paths that led through crooked, elfin ways up the flank of the mountain.

"Huh," said Clay, a few minutes later. "I've never been on this path. I thought I knew all the woods around here! Smart girl!"

They walked up through woods of beech and birch, past the stone foundations of houses that had vanished long before. They walked under huge white pines that had been growing for two hundred years.

They came out in a meadow that looked across the distant hills of green and blue. "Wow," said Clay. "I've never seen this meadow. Cool view." He sat down for a second beside the dog.

He looked down the slope of the hill and across a little valley. About a mile away, there was a village center peeking out through the billowing trees. Clay could see the roofs of a few houses, the white steeple of a church, and the green of some lawns and gardens.

Clay couldn't figure out where he was. He tried to draw a map in his head. He was very good at that. He and his dad often played a game when they were out walking or driving: His dad would stop and point out distant hills and mountains and villages and ask Clay to identify them. His father would say, "If that's Spruce Peak, then what would be next to it?" or "If we're facing north, what lake could that be?" or "The sun is setting over that way. So what direction is that? And what town is over there?" Clay knew the town of Gerenford and the towns around it pretty well. But he couldn't make a mental map to figure out where this little village might be. It was at the bottom of a hill, and maybe that hill was the one called Owl's Head. But Clay didn't know of any houses between Mount Norumbega and Owl's Head. He wished his dad were there to talk it over. They could take out his dad's phone and get a GPS reading and a map to tell them what village was there.

The dog was not paying attention to the distant village. She was poking around the field, sniffing.

"It looks like that village is about a mile away," said Clay. "We're going to walk there from here."

The dog didn't understand exactly what Clay was saying,

but she was very glad they were moving again. She soared along in front of him, running across the field.

Clay was very happy with how the day was going. There are few better things in life than exploring with a dog and finding new places together.

As they walked along, Clay talked to the dog, who bounded ahead. "What is your name?" he wondered. "They better not have given you a dumb name like Fifi. You're too much like a wild queen."

He tried to come up with names. He called them out to see if she liked any of them. "Wendy! . . . Morgan! . . . Balf!" He tried royal names ("Queenie? Majesty? Lady?"), and he tried the names of warrior queens from science fiction movies ("Leia? Aelita? Xena? Zontrad?"). He tried names of girls in his class. He even tried the days of the week, and for a minute she seemed mildly interested in Tuesday, but it turned out to be a pheasant in a bush.

None of the names worked for her.

About twenty minutes later, Clay spotted a house through the trees. It was an old-fashioned farmhouse with a big chimney. They must be at that village. Carefully, he walked through the trees toward the house.

Now he could see the village street, the church on the

green, and the other cottages, the old mill made of stone, a river running under a bridge, the weeping willow trees over the pond.

And somehow he knew something was very wrong. He knew he never should have come to this hidden place. He did not belong. He knew it even before he saw who lived there.

Clay stooped down to hide behind a stump.

Unfortunately, that was just when the dog saw a cat on the lawn and bolted out of hiding to chase it.

Oh no! What was he going to do?

He looked out again. The dog was standing in front of the house's open door, barking furiously. The cat had slipped inside and disappeared.

Someone was going to hear all that racket. Clay had to do something.

He crept behind the wooden wall of a vegetable garden. He could hear voices. He shimmied past the beans and zucchini. *Weird,* he thought. His mom's vegetable plants hadn't even started sprouting yet. How was—

Suddenly the dog stopped barking. That could not be good.

Terrified, Clay sneaked to the edge of the vegetable garden and peeked around the corner. He hid as well as he could in the long grass.

The dog was wagging her tail between two men who stood with their backs to Clay. Something was wrong with them. It took Clay a minute to recognize what it was.

They were dressed in old-fashioned clothes, as if it were still 1800: long brown coats and wide black hats.

They were talking in strange, hissing voices. They were talking about the dog.

"She is a loud one, Cousin Tharpolamew."

"She almost supped upon my cat."

"Is your cat a good mouser?"

The one called Cousin Tharpolamew laughed an odd, raspy laugh. "Not as fine as me."

The other man bent down and petted Clay's dog. She wagged her tail. The man said, "This appears to be one of the royal hunting dogs of the People Under the Mountain."

"Yes, that is what she appears to be, Cousin Odediah."

"Her collar says her name is 'Elphinore.'"

Clay was surprised. He didn't remember seeing any writing on the collar at all. Just all the glass rubies and plastic pearls.

Cousin Tharpolamew said, "Elphinore, hmm?"

"In the runes of that people, it says, 'Elphinore.'"

"Should we return her?"

"I will not go see the People Under the Mountain. They are not kind to us."

Clay was about to protest that, anyway, they had no right to return his dog to anyone. That was his decision.

But when he opened his mouth, he saw something that shut him right up.

At just the sound of his mouth flapping open, one of the men started to turn his head. He did not stop turning his head. His head turned all the way around on his neck.

A face was looking backward toward Clay. It was the face of a huge owl. The eyes were metallic, like gold foil.

The other man's head turned now, too, as in a nightmare. They both were looking toward him. Two owl faces, beaked and feathered, under wide-brimmed hats of black.

Clay crouched down in the long grass. He did not move. He knew owls had good sight. They were used to finding things in grass.

"Your cat is not a good mouser," said Cousin Odediah. "Sometimes there are field mice in your garden."

"They swiftly come to grief," said the other.

"Indeed, cousin. Good day, cousin. I take my leave of you." The man's head swiveled back around, and he walked off toward the village green.

Clay was petrified. He didn't know if by "field mice," they meant him. He didn't know if they had really seen him.

Cousin Tharpolamew was heading right into the vegetable garden. Clay flattened himself against the wooden fence. He could hear the man moving right behind him.

Now, through the long grasses, Clay could see people walking around the village, and he could see that all of them had the heads of owls. They wore old-fashioned clothing of black and brown and white and gray. They went about their village tasks, carrying rakes and baskets and scythes.

There was a clunk behind him. Clay's heart raced. Cousin Tharpolamew was up to something. Clay looked through a crack between the boards. He fought to keep his breath silent.

The owl man had a table of what looked like big wooden salt and pepper shakers in front of him. He selected one of them and walked over to the cabbages. Clicking his beak, he sprinkled something from the shaker all over the cabbage vines.

Now Clay had a new problem. The elf dog—Elphinore—had finished sniffing at the house's stone foundation and was trotting over toward him. She didn't understand that Clay was trying to hide.

He shook his head. She didn't know what that meant.

Another clunk behind Clay: the owl-head man had put down the wooden shaker. He was walking back to the house.

"Run far, elf-hound," the man hissed to the dog. "Forget your masters and run."

The man went inside. The door of the house shut and locked.

Clay braced himself against the fence and caught his breath.

But there was a sound from behind the fence—the sound of something creeping.

Clay fell to the ground and looked quickly through the gap between the planks.

The cabbages were growing. He could actually see them growing as he watched. Leaves were unfurling. Their round, frilly heads were rising from the ground like the heads of the dead.

Clay had to get away. No one would believe what he had seen. He couldn't believe it himself.

He stood up and got ready to run back to the cover of the woods. The dog thought they were going to play. She leaped a little, excited that they were on their way again.

But Clay was looking at the table covered in wooden shakers right on the other side of the fence. The shakers that held the magical plant food that was making the cabbages grow so quickly.

Normally, Clay would never have even thought of stealing. He was not that kind of kid at all.

But somehow, he had to take something back from this miraculous owl town.

He had to show people that it existed, even though it had never been here before.

He had to prove it to himself.

And so he grabbed a wooden shaker, and then he ran as fast as he could toward the trees, toward the forest, toward the paths he knew. Toward home.

Chapter Four

Clay had a plan: when he got home, he was going to tell his mother the story of his adventure, and then, when she didn't believe any of it—about the village that shouldn't exist and the owl-headed gardener—he would pull out the shaker of magical powder, shake it on her vegetable beds that were still just seedlings, and show her how all the plants suddenly grew.

That wasn't what happened, though. Instead, when he got home, she told him to go wash his hands and help her make lunch. Immediately. No argument.

"Can't DiRossi or Dad help? I've got to show you something."

"DiRossi just got up and she's about to take a bath. Your father is doing laundry. He's having a tough day. Mrs.

Haverson keeps calling him saying there's a giant blue lizard in one of the culverts over on Alder Street. Insane."

Clay was in charge of toasting all the bread for the family's sandwiches.

"We still haven't gotten any calls about the dog," said his mother, hunting for mayonnaise.

"Her name's Elphinore," Clay explained.

His mother's head appeared around the fridge door. "How do you know?"

"It says it on her collar."

Clay's mother looked confused. She closed the fridge and walked over to the dog. The red-eared dog was looking up at the lunch meats on the counter like someone at the Eiffel Tower falling in love. Gently, Clay's mom reached out and spun the collar on the dog's neck. "There's nothing written on the collar," she said. "Just all these glitzy symbols."

"They say Elphinore," Clay explained. "In another language. She's a royal dog."

"Honey," said his mother sadly. "Don't get too attached to her. We're going to have to give her back."

"Mom," said Clay, "she's not a normal dog. I'm serious. Look, I got to show you something." It was time to pull out the wooden shaker and amaze his mom with the story of how the dog had led him to the owl-head village. But the shaker wasn't on the kitchen counter. Clay couldn't actually remember where he had put it down when he got home. He looked around the kitchen. It wasn't anywhere. "One sec. Let me find—" he started to say, but he was interrupted by DiRossi's terrified screaming.

Clay and his mom looked up, shocked by the shrieks coming from the bathroom. Then Mrs. O'Brian ran to see what was wrong. Clay followed. From the bathroom, they could already hear furious sloshing and splashing.

Clay's mother threw open the door.

There was DiRossi, soaking wet, shivering, wrapped in a towel she had just grabbed, standing knee-deep in the tub.

And all around her in the tub was marsh grass, as if she were standing in the middle of a pond somewhere.

"What's going on?" she yelled. *"Why is there grass growing in the tub suddenly?"*

She had been relaxing in her bath, head leaned back, eyes closed, when suddenly she'd felt something brushing up against her legs. That's when she had started screaming. When she'd opened her eyes, she found green strands shooting up all around her.

Now she stood there, looking down at the brown, cloudy water and the grasses rustling in the breeze from the open door.

Mr. O'Brian appeared behind Clay. He was a very practical man, and he was never surprised by anything. He saw the bathtub filled with reeds and he frowned. All he said was "That's strange."

"It sure is," said Mrs. O'Brian.

"What about my bath?" complained DiRossi from the tub. "My feet are covered in mud!" Then she shrieked again. *"SOMETHING SLIMY JUST BRUSHED AGAINST MY FOOT!"* She tried picking up one foot, but the other foot was still down in the water. So she switched feet in a clumsy dance. *"NOW MY OTHER FOOT!"*

Juniper walked over and knelt down next to the tub. "It's just a catfish, DiRossi," she said. She wiggled her fingers in the water. "Hello, Mr. Whiskers."

DiRossi made a noise of agonized irritation and marched straight out of the bath, past her sister and brother and parents, and toward her room, leaving a trail of muddy footprints.

"Stay away from the tub until your father checks it out," Mrs. O'Brian warned Juniper. "There might be snapping turtles."

Clay suddenly had an awful idea of where he might have left the wooden shaker. Right before he had started to toast the toast, right before DiRossi had started to take her bath, he had gone into the bathroom to wash his hands.

He looked around the bathroom for the shaker. He didn't see it, but his father was already saying, "Okay, let's go. Let's clear out. I'm closing the door."

Clay went to talk to DiRossi. She was getting dressed in her bedroom. Through the door, Clay said, "DiRossi? Did you . . . did you maybe find a wooden sort of shaker in the bathroom?"

"The one with the bath salts?" said DiRossi. "Yeah. I used them for my bath."

Clay was starting to understand why maybe the tub was suddenly full of pond life. Something about that magic dust.

"Oh," he said to his sister, unhelpfully.

"Clay?" she said. "Does this have to do with the marsh grass in the tub?"

"Hmm," said Clay, as if he hadn't thought of that idea.

Then he decided maybe he better go downstairs before she got all questiony.

Clay's parents and his little sister were looking at something at the kitchen table. They were all huddled together.

Uh-oh. Clay wondered what they were inspecting so carefully.

"Well, what about that," said his father.

"Clay will toast you more bread, honey," Mrs. O'Brian said to Juniper.

Almost afraid to look, Clay sneaked up beside them.

"I used the salt on my sandwich," said Juniper.

And she pointed at the wooden shaker.

Clay looked at her sandwich.

The wheat bread had sprouted actual stalks of wheat. It was like a tiny square of a wheat field. And beside it, the lettuce was crackling quietly as a single leaf grew into a whole head of lettuce.

"It's the shaker that's doing it," whispered Clay. "I found it in the woods. I think it makes things grow. It's like nature plus."

"What *is* this stuff?" said Mr. O'Brian, picking up the shaker. He dumped a little of the powder out onto the table. He squatted down and looked at it closely. "It just looks like salt," he said. "You found the shaker out in the woods? Huh. All sorts of strange things up there. I wonder what this is."

And then, as they watched, the oak table began to grow a branch. It was a small branch, with delicate little leaves on it. The leaves unfurled, as if spring were turning to summer. They were oak leaves.

"Look," said Juniper. "An acorn!"

"Well, I'll be dagnabbed," said Mr. O'Brian.

"It's Nature Plus," Clay repeated, awestruck. "It makes things super-grow."

"We should do experiments!" said Juniper. "To see what turns into what!"

"I'm the one who found it," said Clay. "I brought it back for Mom and Dad to use in the garden so we could have vegetables."

But Juniper had already grabbed it from the table and started sprinkling the powder all over her sweater. "Let's see what it does to me!" she said.

"No!" said Clay. "Watch out!" and his mother said, "Junie, honey, that doesn't seem like a good—"

But then they shut up in amazement. Juniper's sweater was changing. It was getting lumpy.

"It's growing more wool!" Juniper said in delight. "Look how fuzzy it is!"

"Yes, sir, yes, sir, three bags full," Mr. O'Brian joked, which nobody thought was funny. Because now the sweater was moving.

"Get out of the sweater!" cried Clay. "It's alive!"

And indeed, as Juniper struggled to take off the sweater, a small head had started to appear in the middle of her back. A sheep's head.

"Help me!" she exclaimed, and Clay rushed to help her, and everyone started yelling advice, including the elf dog, who was barking furiously at the blinking sheep.

The sheep's legs were growing out all over the sweater. The sheep was not particularly sheep-shaped. For one thing, there were five legs poking in different directions. For another thing, there were sleeves. Juniper struggled to free herself, crying, "I'm in a sheep! Help me get out of this sheep!"

The dog danced around her, barking warning.

Clay tugged.

Juniper flew backward, free.

The weird sheep-sweater landed on the floor and started to walk around drunkenly. It was much smaller than a normal sheep, being just larger than a child's sweater. It was also confused, having five legs and two sleeves that dragged along the floor.

It expected to be in a field full of clover, not in a kitchen, surrounded by gobsmacked humans, barked at by a furious hunting dog.

"What's going on?" DiRossi yelled down from her room.

"There's a sheep," her mother called back up, a little uncertainly.

"No," said DiRossi. "I mean in the laundry room? It sounds like the washer's broken."

"The laundry room?" said Mrs. O'Brian. She asked her husband, "Weren't you just washing your work clothes?"

"Yeah," said Mr. O'Brian. "And yes, if you're wondering, I used that powder. I saw the shaker in the bathroom and I thought it was some kind of fancy detergent you were trying." The family looked at him in terror. "Don't worry," he said. "My overalls are made of cotton. Worst thing that could happen is the laundry room will be full of cotton bushes."

But then, from the laundry room, the family heard a small roar.

"And my work shirt," said Mr. O'Brian. "No problem there. It's a polyester blend."

"What's polyester made from?" asked Juniper.

"It's like plastic," Clay explained.

Mr. O'Brian said, "I guess it's made from petroleum, you could say."

"What's petroleum made from?" asked Juniper.

"It's oil," said Clay.

"What's oil made from?" asked Juniper.

And Clay said, "Long-dead stuff. From really long ago."

There was another little roar from the laundry room.

"Like dinosaurs," said Clay.

Chapter Five

The O'Brian family approached the door to the laundry room with caution. There were no more roars. It was silent.

Mr. O'Brian was carrying a fireplace poker. Mrs. O'Brian was brandishing a fire extinguisher.

Clay got to the side of the laundry room door and waited for his mom and dad to give the order to open it.

"Ready?" said Mr. O'Brian.

Clay nodded.

"Go!"

Clay threw the door open.

The little room was silent. They all looked in.

Mr. O'Brian's cotton pants had turned into cotton plants. They had bashed open the front of the washer. They had still been spinning as they grew, so the branches and stems stuck out in wild, tangled spirals, covered in cotton tufts. It looked like a wooden tornado, complete with crazy clouds. It filled most of the room.

And that meant that it hid whatever Mr. O'Brian's polyester work shirt had turned into. Now that the door was open, they could hear something scrabbling in the corner. Something was hiding in the cotton.

The elf-hound stalked forward. She knew just what to do. This was her specialty: hunting little monsters in weird, otherworldly forests.

"Elphinore," said Clay. "I don't think that's a good idea."

She growled at whatever was lurking in the corner.

"What kind of name is that?" said Mr. O'Brian.

The dog crept forward, a river of hair on her back bristling.

The cotton plants rustled.

The hunting dog lowered her head and raised her lip in a snarl.

Then the dinosaur rushed out, roaring.

It was a small dinosaur—about the size of a chicken— with four stumpy legs, two floppy sleeves, a mean tyrannosaurus face, a spiked tail, and Clay's dad's name, *Barry*, sewed in cursive on its hip.

The hunting dog and the shirt-o-saur faced off. They circled each other in the shadows of the whirlwind cotton trees.

They struck so fast, the family couldn't even follow the fight. Each little beast lunged toward the other, snapping.

"No!" said Clay. He didn't want Elphinore to get hurt—but he also wanted to save the dinosaur, since it was the only one around for the last billion years or so.

He watched in horror as the creatures nipped at each other. Elphinore was savage.

The dinosaur made a break for it. It dashed out between their legs.

"Grab it!" Clay's mom yelled, but no one was going to grab a dinosaur, even one the size of a short-sleeved shirt.

Then they heard the sweater-sheep bleat in surprise.

"He's gonna eat my sweater!" yelped Juniper.

What followed was a wild chase through the house. The sheep ran as fast as its five legs could carry it, tripping over its own sleeves. The shirt-o-saurus followed the sheep, roaring in soprano. Elphinore chased the dinosaur. And the family chased Elphinore, all of them dodging around tables, chairs, and the sectional sofa.

Who knows who would have won this race, this hectic parade of evolution, if Juniper hadn't opened the front door and yelled, "RUN, SWEATER-SHEEP! RUN!"

The sheep hightailed it out the door. Juniper swung the door shut, trying to slam it closed—but she wasn't fast enough. The dinosaur wriggled through, growling, and took off across the lawn.

Elphinore was furious. How could these people stop her from killing that little monster? She barked and barked at the door, ran to the windows, and stood up on her hind legs, watching the sheep and the dino bumble toward the woods. She punched the window glass with her forepaws.

Juniper was heartbroken. "My sheep," she said. "That dinosaur is going to kill and eat my first sheep."

The family looked out at the forest in wonder at everything that had just happened.

"Quiet that dog down," said Mrs. O'Brian.

"Her name's Elphinore," insisted Clay.

Strange to say, the dinosaur did not eat the sheep. Perhaps they sensed a distant kinship because they both had been clothing once. Maybe it was just that the dinosaur couldn't chew through all that wool.

For years afterward, people would claim they saw a little dinosaur and a mutant sheep in the forest around Mount Norumbega: an unlikely couple, predator and prey.

The dinosaur was cold-blooded and found the snowy winters difficult. During those times, he would wear the sheep like a sweater. They would wander through the solemn white woods, one head pointing each way. They would sleep curled up together for warmth, and the dinosaur, eyes half-closed, would gently chew on the sheep, purring.

The O'Brians would have been pleased to know that their shirt-and-sweater set would be happy and comfortable together for years to come. But they were thinking more about that wooden shaker and its magical crystal salts with the power of Nature Plus.

"Do we try it on the garden?" said Mrs. O'Brian.

Clay wasn't sure anymore.

"If this was a fairy tale," said Juniper, "it would be dangerous to dump it all over the garden, and that would lead to all kinds of messes and disasters, and we would learn our lesson."

"But it's not a fairy tale," said Mrs. O'Brian, "and we could maybe get the garden to grow half of the food we need this summer. It would be a real help."

Before anyone could protest, she walked out the door with the shaker and began dusting all the tiny shoots that were just coming up in the vegetable beds.

She only got around a few of the beds before she ran out of powder. They had used a lot in the bath, the washer, the sandwich, and Juniper's sweater. But the plants it touched flourished. They stretched their limbs and yawned. The bean vines corkscrewed their way up the stakes. Down along the ground, green coils shrugged, and zucchinis were born. Tomatoes swelled like water balloons.

It went on for five minutes, and then it all stopped. The garden was all set. In just a few minutes, it had gone from looking like May to looking like July.

It seemed like a very good sign that this would be an excellent summer.

So why did Clay feel so worried?

That night, he dreamed horrible dreams: that the house was filled with wild growth, things sprouting everywhere. He saw terrible eyes glaring through the stalks and leaves. Panthers were crouching at the top of the stairs. And all around him, there was an eerie hooting; there were stealthy footsteps on the roof. Even in his dreams, he reached out to put his hand on Elphinore, who was sleeping beside his bed. When she felt his hand, she licked his wrist.

He dreamed of thornbushes in the living room strangling his sisters.

He woke up sleepy, as if he hadn't slept at all.

And a few minutes later, when he let Elphinore out to go pee, he saw her sniffing and pawing something on the edge of the woods: an ugly little disk of bones and hair.

"Uhh!" he exclaimed. "What's this?"

DiRossi came over to see what he was talking about. "Oh, that's nothing," she said. "It's what owls spit up after they eat a mouse or something. It's called an owl pellet."

It stared up at him from the forest floor like an evil eye—a warning or a curse.

Chapter Six

"What is Clay's weird little secret?" DiRossi asked Juniper the morning after Nature Plus.

"You mean where he got the dog and the magic salt?"

"Yeah. And why he got so strange when I told him what an owl pellet was. He ran to Mom and was like 'Oh, oh, oh, Mom, I have to skip my school stuff today. I have something I have to do. I got to go to the forest. Wah, wah, wah.'" She rubbed fake tears with her fists.

"That doesn't sound like Clay's voice," said Juniper.

"It's what his brain would sound like if it could talk," said DiRossi, who was sick of her sister and brother.

DiRossi was even angrier about being trapped at home by the worldwide sickness than Clay was. School online would be over soon. It would be the beginning of summer. She was fourteen, and she wanted to spend the summer with her friends: it was their turn as fourteen-year-olds to spend long, lazy weeks riding their skateboards around the church parking lot, going to get veggie burgers at the diner, and sitting on the town green near the pioneer statue, laughing at dumb jokes. She had seen bigger kids doing all this stuff from the time she was little. It was *her turn* as a fourteen-year-old. She would only have one fourteen-year-old summer. And instead, she had to spend it stuck at home with her family. It wasn't fair.

"Why don't you like our family anymore?" asked Juniper.

"Because you're all weird."

"Why are we weird?" Juniper asked. "I'm very orderly and normal."

"Our brother is afraid of owl vomit. Our dad got up at dawn to go fishing in the bathroom."

Mr. O'Brian had caught two nice-size catfish and a trout in the tub. He was going to fry them up for dinner.

Juniper suggested, "We could follow Clay when he goes out this afternoon and see where he goes." She hoped her sister thought it was a really good idea.

DiRossi nodded. "I want to see where he got that shaker of Nature Plus. And I bet that's where he's going." She headed upstairs. "I'm going to my room. Wake me up when he's ready to leave."

Her room was dark and safe like a cave. If she couldn't be hanging out on the town green with her friends, she wanted to be sitting in the dark, angry and miserable. It was good to feel like a furnace of anger that heated the whole house until no one was comfortable and everyone was sweating. She threw herself down on her bed and texted her friend Euj, short for Eugene, about how her family was all stupid and weird, except for her, and her dad had actually worn his rubber boots to go fishing in the bathroom.

A little after lunch, Clay finished his schoolwork, and Juniper noticed her brother looking sneaky. He went over to the kitchen counter where their mom had left the wooden shaker and he swiped it. He stuck it in his backpack. When he saw Juniper staring at him, he froze for a second in shock, then ran for the front door, yelling a vague "Bye!" to their mother.

He whispered, "Come on, Elphinore!" and the dog leaped off the couch and followed him outside.

Juniper ran up the stairs and knocked lightly on DiRossi's door. It was an emergency, but she knew DiRossi got angry if people knocked too loud, as if her family was a headache she always had.

DiRossi was sitting cross-legged on her bed, listening to sad virus music. Normally, she would have screamed at Juniper to leave her alone, but this was important. She wanted to know what magical place Clay had found in the forest.

She and Juniper waited until Clay headed up the path. "We want to keep far enough away from him so he can't see us, but close enough that we can hear him," said DiRossi.

"You're talking about strategy with the right person," said Juniper, very proud.

DiRossi hissed, "Keep it down."

They cautiously started into the woods, following the same path as Clay.

Juniper said in a stage whisper, "You don't have to wear sunglasses. If he sees us, he's going to recognize you anyway."

"It's so my world is always in shadow," said DiRossi. "It's always midnight for me, Juniper."

"Okay," said Juniper. "I thought we were giving each other spy advice."

They walked silently for a few minutes. The new leaves had just unfurled a couple of days before, and they were still a light, young green.

DiRossi grabbed her sister's shoulder and stopped them both in their tracks so they could listen.

Far ahead, they could hear Clay tramping through the woods. He was talking to Elphinore. "We've got to get this back to them, Elphinore," he said. "You got to show me the way to their village. Which way, girl?"

Juniper wondered, "Whose village?"

DiRossi had no idea. But she wanted to find out.

Clay was pleading with the dog. "Which way is it? This is where we left the path last time. You knew another path. Which way, girl?"

They could hear the dog frisking around him.

"We'll play in a minute, but first, lead me to that meadow. Remember? And that town?"

"He's talking to a dog," said DiRossi. "That's what I mean when I say my family's weird."

Juniper looked at her with scorn. "She's a smart dog," said Juniper protectively.

The sisters followed the sound of their brother through the woods. They followed a path up a slope, toward the mountain.

They came to a circle of giant stones in the woods. The stones were covered with moss.

DiRossi walked between the giant stones, amazed. They looked like something from a fantasy game she would play, like you were supposed to have martial arts battles in the center of the circle. "Cool!" she said, taking out her phone to photograph them. "I never even knew these were here!"

She lifted her phone. On three of the closest stones sat owls, staring down at the girls.

It was an amazing picture, if she could get it. She clicked the phone on.

The owls lifted off and flew into the forest.

DiRossi sighed and dropped her phone into her pocket. Opportunity missed.

Far ahead, up the slope, she heard Clay calling the dog.

Elphinore was leading him up the slope of Mount Norumbega. The farther up she went, the more excited she got. Clay gave up on finding the lost village again for the moment. He was excited to see where Elphinore would lead him next. He knew that she was somehow bringing him to places that he never could have reached on his own. He looked up the slope of the mountain.

"What's up there, girl? Huh?" he said.

She grinned and leaped, racing forward and then circling back for him.

Elphinore wondered why the human boy was not more excited. They were near the entrance to her kingdom! They were almost home!

The boy also did not seem to know that the two girls were following behind. Those girls would get very lost if they weren't herded in the right direction. They couldn't see the hidden paths. Elphinore was eager to race ahead, but instead she galloped back to the girls and steered them onto the right path. The little one ran after her with outstretched arms, yelling her name. But Elphinore didn't have time to stop. Her brothers and sisters were close now—waiting for her to return! She ran back up to the boy, who was looking for her.

She led him to the entrance of the Kingdom Under the Mountain. She waited for him to open the magical gate and let her in.

Clay stood and looked where the dog had brought him: it was a blank cliff. Nothing but rough granite. Why had she brought him here?

Elphinore walked forward and pawed the face of the cliff. She looked at him, whining as if she were asking him a favor. She pawed the rock again. Then Clay figured out what was going on. She scratched at the cliff as if she wanted to be let into the mountain.

It was where she was from.

"Don't you want to stay with me?" he asked. "You don't want to go back down there. Under the mountain."

She started wildly digging, as if everything she cared about could be uncovered if she just tunneled deep enough.

"Elphinore," said Clay. "Please, girl."

She didn't pay any attention to him. It was as if she had already forgotten him.

He remembered the owl-head men talking about how she belonged to "the People Under the Mountain."

No, she belonged with him. He knew it. But apparently she didn't. She was waiting for him to perform some kind of magic so she could go home—to her real home.

Her miraculous visit was over. She was going to go back underground and disappear forever. Clay couldn't believe she didn't choose him instead. "Just try to stay with me," he pleaded. "Just for a little while."

And then he looked up and found his sisters standing there behind him. He didn't even bother to be angry that they had followed him. He just said, "She wants to go back. She doesn't want to stay with me."

"Go back where?" DiRossi asked, looking up the height of the cliff. Bushes and pines hung over the top twenty feet above them.

"To the People Under the Mountain," said Clay. Then he said to DiRossi, "Go ahead and make a joke about how nobody wants to stay with me because I smell bad. Go ahead. I don't care."

DiRossi looked surprised because she had in fact been about to make that exact joke. But he looked so miserable she didn't say a thing.

"Doesn't Elphinore want to stay with us?" Juniper asked, kneeling down to inspect the dog.

"With me," said Clay, sadly. "She doesn't want to stay with me."

Elphinore's purple claws scratched against the granite. She sniffed at the blueberry bushes that grew around the bottom of the cliff as if she could smell her brothers and sisters there.

DiRossi said, "Is this where you found that salt shaker?"

"That was the village of the owl-head people," said Clay, without explanation. He called to Elphinore, "Come on, Elphinore. Let's go home." He wanted to get her away from the mountain.

But she just sat there on her haunches, staring at him, as if he knew how to open a door in the side of a mountain. She trusted him.

"No, we're not going in there," said Clay. "We're going home." Then he corrected himself: "Well, my home. Don't you want to, Elphinore?"

Clay looked so heartbroken that the dog walked to him and licked him on the nose. He reached up, and for the first time, she let him scratch her head. She tilted her head so he would scratch the best spots. She looked adoringly into his eyes.

When he had finished scratching behind her pointed ears, he stood up.

She looked at him with great sympathy. He could see it in her eyes. But it was like she was saying, *Don't worry. You'll remember how to open the gate and take us down to the world underground.*

That was where she belonged.

He thought it was better to ignore that. He said a final "Let's go, girl." It took all his strength, but he turned away from her and just started walking home the way they had come. He didn't even look back to see if Elphinore followed him.

She still sat by the cliff. She watched him walk away.

"Come on," DiRossi whispered to the red-eared dog, as if just by wanting, she could make the dog follow her miserable brother.

As if she'd understood the command, Elphinore rose and trotted after the boy.

The sisters followed.

Juniper, of course, had questions. "I have about a million questions!" she announced loudly to the whole forest. "Actually, seven. First, who are the owl-head people? Second, who put those giant rocks in a circle down there? Clay? Third—"

DiRossi put her arm around her sister. "Shh," she said. "Clay doesn't want to answer questions. And it's better not to ask. The stones in the circle could be the kind of stones that jump around at night and squash little girls flat. So their little-girl brains come out between their teeth."

Juniper glared at her sister.

"It's a geological fact," said DiRossi.

The three kids and the dog walked away through the forest, their voices getting fainter through the trees.

Behind them, a figure stepped out of the woods onto the path. A pair of golden owl eyes watched them disappear. Then quietly, the figure followed them, his dark suit blending with the bark and fallen leaves.

Chapter Seven

The house was dark. It was long after midnight. Everyone slept in their beds. Someone walked across the lawn.

Clay woke up, startled: Elphinore was barking viciously. She stood in the middle of the room, glaring out the window.

"Oh, dog," said Juniper, and she put her pillow over her head.

"What's going on?" said Clay. "Is there something out there?"

The dog pawed at the bedroom door. She wanted to go downstairs.

Clay let her into the hall. She loped down the steps and scrambled through the house, looking out all the windows. She started barking again. Something was lurking outside. She could smell it.

"What's going on, Clay?" his mom called from their bedroom.

"Nothing," said Clay. "Just the dog."

But he was nervous. He went down to see what she was barking at.

Clay followed Elphinore from room to room. But the world outside the windows was pitch-black.

Then she stopped her barking and froze, looking out the living room window, one paw raised.

Clay could not believe how silent the whole house was. The only sound was the new moths thumping faintly against the glass of the back door.

Boom. The motion-sensor light went on in the yard. It glared so bright that Clay could see every shrub and blade of grass.

And right in the center of the lawn, staring at the house, was the outline of a figure with the head of an owl.

Clay and the figure stared at each other. Clay was so terrified he could not move.

The figure walked toward the window, making movements with its arms.

Clay backed up, away from the window.

But as he watched the figure, he saw that it was waving at him. He also saw that it was very short. Much shorter

than the owl-head men he had seen two days before in the village.

It was an owl-head child.

It shielded its eyes with its hands to see despite the glare.

It pointed to Clay and it crooked its finger: *Come here.*

For some reason, Clay went to the front door. He opened the door and let the dog out.

It was an owl-head boy dressed in black, like for a funeral.

Elphinore streaked across the lawn. The owl boy flinched, but held out the back of his hand for Elphinore to sniff.

The dog slowed to a walk and circled him, sniffing.

Clay trusted her judgment. He went out to talk to the owl boy.

"I am Amos," said the owl boy. "I do not like the light."

"Around the side of the house," said Clay. The owl boy followed him.

They stood in the shadow of the house, several feet apart. Elphinore sat in between them, watching the owl boy carefully.

Amos the owl boy said, "It would be better if you gave me the shaker."

"I tried to get it back to your town," said Clay. "I'm sorry. It's all out of powder."

The owl boy said, "When I return it to Brother Tharpolamew, I will lay it down on its side under the table in his garden. He will think it fell."

"How did you know I had it?" asked Clay.

"I saw you from my window."

"Did they see me? The owl-head men?"

"Yes. But they did not know you stole. If they knew, they would be angry. They would come out of the woods and curse your house."

"I'll go in and get it," said Clay. "One sec." He ran inside and up to his room to get the shaker. Because it was cold out, he also put on shoes and a jacket.

When he got back outside, Amos was still waiting in the shadows behind the lilac.

"I'm really sorry," said Clay.

"You should not take from other worlds. If the People Under the Mountain knew you had their hunting hound, they would destroy your house and everyone in it. They do not like human beings."

Clay looked down at the dog, sitting so protectively in front of him. She was a wonderful dog. He wasn't going to give her up.

"If the People Under the Mountain took care of her right, she wouldn't have run away," he said. "She likes it here."

The owl boy said, "She was scratching to get back into the mountain. I saw you both. She does not belong here in this world."

Clay wanted to yell at the owl boy. He didn't want to think about his dog whining to be locked in a cave.

Clay's mother had said that when a guest was rude, you should politely change the subject. Clay wondered what his mom and dad would say to a visiting owl child. He tried, "Would you like a glass of water or some peanut butter crackers?"

Amos said, "Among my kind, the polite thing is to lead your guest first to your basement. It is dark and cool there, and it shows you are willing to offer the pick of all your rodents."

"Rodents? Like mice and rats?"

"And voles."

"Okay," said Clay, "but shhh. Don't wake up my mom and dad." He went over to the basement bulkhead and swung the door open wide. The two of them went down the steps into the basement. It smelled comfortably of mildew and growth. There were boxes of forgotten things all around them. There were machines no one ever used.

Elphinore was delighted there was a new place in the house to explore. She pranced down the steps and snuffled along the floor.

Clay sat on an old lawn chair. Amos was rooting around over near the gardening tools.

"Do you go to school?" Clay asked.

"Yes," said Amos. "There are twelve of us who go to the schoolhouse in our village. I did not want them to know about you, though. None of us has spoken to a human-head person before." He sat down across from Clay. A small tail twirled in his beak as he swallowed a mouse. He looked toward the ceiling. Clay could see the lump dropping down his throat.

Clay winced. "Was that a good one?"

"Dusty," said Amos.

"How do you keep hidden from us?" Clay asked.

"We and your people are in different folds of space. You must have followed your dog to find us. She is trained to see all the paths that lead between impossible places."

"What else is out there that I've never seen before?"

"Those woods are full of hidden things," said Amos. "Some of them are kind. Some of them are dangerous. They are all inches away, but you cannot see them, and usually they cannot see you."

"Like the People Under the Mountain?"

"They are an ancient and dangerous crowd." The owl child stood. "I should return to the village," he said. "I will take the shaker and lay it in the weeds in Tharpolamew's garden."

"I really shouldn't have taken it."

Amos shrugged. "I liked you more because you were daring."

He walked up the steps to the lawn.

Clay thought about his boring, trapped life during the sickness and said, "Want to hang out some time?"

"Yes," said Amos. "I will see you in the wood tomorrow. We can go visit some of the wonders."

Then Amos walked away into the night.

Clay closed the bulkhead doors to the basement. Elphinore was strolling around the yard, looking for more intruders.

Clay stood there for a minute, then went inside.

The next morning, when Clay talked to Levi on the computer, Levi was full of news: "The funniest thing happened. My mom got her hand caught in the door." Levi grinned. "Crazy!" he said. "It almost made a crunching sound. What's going on there?"

Clay thought about everything that had happened since he talked to Levi the last time: the owl-head village. The shirt-o-saurus and sweater-sheep. The owl child.

For some reason, he did not want to tell Levi about any of it. He felt bad, but he wanted to protect the stories somehow.

"Nothing," he said. "Nothing much going on."

He counted the minutes before he could run back to the woods with his dog and, with the owl boy, see the forest's hidden wonders.

CHAPTER EIGHT

The right time to start out on a hike with a new friend is in the morning, when the day still doesn't have anything written on it, when there are no lines drawn on it. Then the day's adventures stretch off into the unseen.

But Clay had to get through the morning's schoolwork, which was terrible, because he and his sisters fought over the computer, calling each other names, and then DiRossi said he was the worst brother ever and stomped off to her room, where she started playing anger music so loud the floors bounced, and—even worse—this meant that Clay had actually won the computer for the morning. He was secretly hoping, of course, that he'd lose the fight, and so DiRossi would be using the computer, so he wouldn't be able to sign on to his class chats. Then he could say to his mom, "Oh, wow, I'm so angry, DiRossi's using the computer and I can't do my math. I guess I'll just go out and explore with the dog."

As he sat there multiplying fractions on the screen, he started to suspect that DiRossi kind of had the same plan for avoiding work as he did, and by losing the fight, she had secretly won. The singer in her music screamed, *"I'm on rage patrol! Rage patrol, marching in lines!"* Her mother called up the stairs, "If you don't turn that down, DiRossi, I'm shutting off the circuit breakers, and it'll all go silent up there."

Clay watched the minutes tick by slowly on the computer screen. Nothing could make them go faster. Elphinore sat curled next to him on the sofa, staring at him with accusing eyes. She didn't understand that he was trapped inside, too. Her eyes said, *We could be exploring beyond all the old stone walls.*

So as soon as it was lunch—as soon as Clay had plastered together a turkey sandwich—he grabbed it off the plate and ran for the woods with the miraculous dog at his side.

She was thrilled they were heading out on an adventure. She leaped at his side, snapping at his wrists and his turkey sandwich with rambunctious joy.

Clay realized that he hadn't set a time or a place to meet Amos the Owl Boy. Once he was far enough into the woods that he wouldn't be heard by his family, he yelled Amos's name a few times.

Elphinore led Clay to the standing stones. Clay didn't want to go any farther—he knew that if they kept going, she would lead him back to that stupid cliff that led into the mountain. So he sat down. "We'll stay here," he announced.

Elphinore was surprised they weren't continuing up the path, but she was perfectly content to run back and forth between the stones, smelling the traces of things from other worlds that had appeared in the middle of the circle long ago.

Clay ate his sandwich and threw Elphinore sticks for a half hour or so. Then the owl child appeared. He was dressed in a small tweed suit that only went down to his knees. His legs were human legs, though. That was a little disappointing: Clay had hoped they would be claws.

"Hello, Clay Human-Head," said Amos, in his strange, formal way, with his small, raspy voice. "I'm glad we found each other."

"I'm ready to explore!" said Clay.

"There are many wonderful things to see." The owl child

stretched out his hand to Elphinore for sniffing. "Should we follow her and see where she takes us?"

"Naw," said Clay. "She wants to go up the mountain. We went there yesterday."

The owl boy looked at him with piercing golden eyes and said nothing.

Clay said, "It's too hot to walk uphill. Let's go look at something else."

"You don't want to go where she wants to lead you," said the owl boy.

"It's a dumb place," said Clay, casually. "Just a cliff. A dead end."

"You know it is not a dead end, Brother Clay."

"Look," said Clay, "is there other stuff to see or isn't there?"

"There is," said Amos, elaborately nodding his feathered head.

"Let's go!"

They rambled through the woods. They talked a little about random things. Clay asked if owls learned how to multiply fractions. Amos said that owl-head children often spent their mathematics classes listening to sounds played on machines, and calculating how far away things were, like a mouse in the long grass. "It is a science studied by the professoriat of bats," he said. "They have created the machines to teach us owls how to hear mathematically."

The two of them threw sticks to Elphinore, which she almost never returned: she galloped into the woods with them in frantic excitement and left them under trees she liked. The three of them wandered along through the forest until they came to the shores of a little sparkling lake surrounded by pines. On the far side there was a slope with apple trees in blossom. "This is the wishing lake," said Amos. "It is fed by the River of Time and Shadow. If you stand on the opposite shore, where the apple trees grow, you can make a wish and it will come true."

"What?" said Clay. "Let's go! Come on!" He started to think of all the things he'd wish for: another laptop, maybe— oh, or maybe some medicine for the sickness that had spread all over the world and shut everything down.

"It is not so easy, Brother Clay," said the owl child. "For a wish to come true on the other side of the lake, a wish has to be taken away from someone on this side of the lake."

"Oh," said Clay, disappointed. "Do you have any dumb wishes you wouldn't mind losing?"

"They have to be real wishes," said the owl child.

"What would you wish for?" Clay asked.

"That my village would never be found by the human-headed people. Also, a stampede of lemmings. They are delicious in pies. They taste tangy, like hysteria." He said, "Let's go see the Sleepers."

As they walked up and down through dark ravines and golden hollows, Clay asked, "Why are you worried about humans finding your village?"

"We must remain hidden. We spend a lot of time walking around the edges of our fields, casting spells so that our village cannot be entered by the people of your world. If you had been an adult and had been seen hiding behind the vegetable garden, your life would have been in danger."

"Just for walking there?"

"The human-head people never simply walk somewhere. They always burn and flatten."

"That's not fair to say," said Clay.

Amos did not answer him.

Irritated, Clay said, "Also, stop calling us 'the human-head people'!"

Amos said, "But you have the bodies of people with the heads of humans."

Clay couldn't read the expression on Amos's owl face. It was hard to tell if a beak was smiling or frowning. Clay couldn't tell what Amos was thinking, or if Amos was even having a good time.

Clay said, "If humans are so bad, then why are you allowed to hang around with one?"

The owl boy turned his head backward to look right at him, still walking forward. "But I am not allowed to be here," he said. "I sneaked away. No one knows that I am here. I could get paddled for disobeying if my parents found out."

"You risked getting in trouble to come see me?"

"Of course," said Amos. "No other boy has ever befriended a human-head person before. Someday I will be able to tell the story."

This made Clay feel a little bit better.

The owl child announced, "Here is a tower that belongs to the Kingdom Under the Mountain."

Clay forgot to be irritated at Amos's comments about humanity. He was amazed to see the ruins of a turret, like the tower of a castle, sticking up from the rocks in the middle of the forest. It looked like cannons had shot parts of it away long ago.

Clay walked into the ruins through a hole in the wall. The inside was filled with bushes. Clay looked up. The tower was an empty shell. "Wow," he said.

"The People Under the Mountain built it when they were at war with a people from another world."

Clay said, "Cool." He stood in the middle of the tower and listened. Over the birdsong and the sound of the wind in the trees, he could hear a faint echo of something else: a distant ringing, a single note, like a finger rubbed around the rim of a glass. "Do you hear that sound?" he asked.

"Yes," said the owl child. "There is always that sound here. There is a legend that during the great war between the People Under the Mountain and invaders from another place, a prince threw himself from the top of this tower when he saw that he was going to lose the battle. One of his military sorcerers tried to save him by opening up a magical door underneath him so the prince would fall through it and wouldn't break all his bones when he hit the ground. Unfortunately, it was a hasty plan. The door led nowhere. The prince fell into the hole and kept falling. They say that the prince falls eternally through space, always trapped in that one moment of falling, and that note is his frozen scream as he falls."

"Whoa," said Clay. He felt a little shiver.

"Do not feel sad for the People Under the Mountain. They are not kind. And don't forget," said the owl boy, "they will destroy your house if they discover that you are keeping their dog." He pointed at Elphinore, who was walking around the outside of the tower, admiring its height and strength.

"They're not going to notice she's gone," said Clay stubbornly. "And she likes staying with me."

Amos didn't answer but started walking again. Clay walked after him, calling, "If you're so good at hearing how far away things are, how far away is the falling prince? Huh?"

Amos said, "Infinitely far away and infinitely near."

Clay rolled his eyes—he was getting a little sick of Amos knowing all about the forest's mysteries—but he didn't want to be rude to a new friend.

Instead, he said, "My dad has a metal detector. He uses it for work. Maybe one time we could bring it out here and look for treasure in the ruins of the tower."

Amos stopped and turned his head backward. "That would be enjoyable," he said. "Now walk onward."

They hadn't gone very far when the owl boy said, "Here is the first Sleeper." He pointed. At first, Clay couldn't see anything but a long, low mound covered with trees.

Then he saw that the mound was in the shape of a giant man lying on his back. Oaks and dark fir trees grew out of his head and stomach. As they walked onward, they passed several more giant men and women, all of them asleep, some on their backs, some on their sides, all of them overgrown with blackberry bushes and the silver trunks of beech trees.

"Who are they?" Clay whispered.

"You do not have to whisper," said the owl child. "They have slept through storms and wars."

Clay watched Elphinore poking around on one of the giant mossy faces. She started to dig near the nose. The body did not move.

"Are you sure they aren't dead?"

"Once or twice a year, one of them breathes. It is a night for celebration. The people of the wood all gather for a ceremony and play them fanfares and lullabies." The owl child climbed up onto the sleeping figure. "If you put your ear to the ground, you can sometimes hear their heart beat once."

"Cool," said Clay, and he climbed up onto the giant's chest to listen.

Elphinore had decided that the giant's nostril was a fox's den or a deadly wyrm's burrow. She was digging furiously with her front paws, throwing a spray of dirt up behind her.

Clay sat down on the fallen leaves and lily of the valley and put his ear to the ground. He waited for a *thump*, a *lub*, or a *dub*.

He and Amos couldn't hear much, though, because Elphinore was standing in the entrance of the nostril as if it were a cave, barking wildly. Her barks echoed in the giant's old stone skull.

"Quiet, Elphinore," said Clay.

"Quiet, sweet one," said Amos.

"Quiet!"

She kept barking and barking at the cave she'd uncovered. Clay started to wonder if something was there—maybe a bear hibernating up the giant's nose.

He started to say, "I can't hear anything over—" but then he was interrupted because the ground shook. "Was that the heart-beat?" he said, excited. But before he could even finish asking, the ground shook again—and again. The trees were wagging. The moss was quivering.

The owl child blinked in astonishment, dropping to his knees.

"Uh-oh," said Clay. "I think Elphinore woke the giant up."

The mound was moving like someone struggling to sit up under heavy blankets. A moan rose all around them. The moan of something that had slept beneath the soil since the last ice age.

"Jump!" said Clay as the dirt under their feet started to shift and roll. Clay and the owl child leaped off the restless giant.

The elf dog did not want to give up the fight, so she still stood on the giant's face, barking up the nose, though right behind her, the stone lips were writhing in a yawn.

"Elphinore!" yelled Clay in warning as he and Amos ran for safety. "Come on, girl!" He was terrified she would tumble into the pit of the giant's mouth and be swallowed.

The dog looked behind her and gave a surprised yip. She leaped off the face and ran after the two boys as the whole head turned to the side.

The giant's eyes were open. The earth had fallen off of much of his face and neck. Beneath the mud, his skin was blue and scaled. He stared at the three small creatures who had woken him. He blinked slowly.

"Your dog," he said in a deep, deep voice, "woke me up."

The forest was silent. The birds had stopped singing. Elphinore had stopped barking.

Clay said, "Sorry?"

"The curse is lifted," said the giant. "I am awake."

Thank goodness, thought Clay. *We just lifted a curse.*

The owl child walked forward and bowed. "Great one," he said, "we greet you. We are happy you once again can walk upon the earth."

The giant said, "Why should anyone be happy? I have no wish to rise and walk. Where would I walk?" He sighed sadly in the long tunnel of his throat. "The world I knew probably disappeared ten thousand years ago." He rolled his eyes around, looking at the tiny people, the tiny trees. "I want to go back to sleep."

Clay said, "If you've been sleeping that long, there's lots of cool stuff you haven't seen though. And you'll be a celebrity. They'll take pictures of you next to the Statue of Liberty."

"You could haunt the wood," Amos suggested. "And become one of the great mysteries of the mountain."

"I could lie here," said the giant, "and lament everything that no longer exists." He closed his eyes.

"What was the world like when you fell asleep?" Clay asked him eagerly. "And who put the curse on you?"

"I can still hear you," said the giant, "which means you haven't gone away yet."

"Should we leave, great one?" Amos asked, and Clay said, "You just woke up! It's a new day!"

The giant exhaled sadly and turned his head to face the other way. He lay under the forest floor like someone in a sleeping bag. Beech trees rose and fell with his breath.

The two boys waited for the giant to do something else.

"I am not moving," said the giant.

They waited longer, but the giant ignored them.

Finally, Amos and Clay sneaked off. "Well, at least he's

breathing more now," Clay said. "You can have more breathing parties."

"I am disappointed," said the owl child. "I thought meeting with a mighty being from the beginning of time would make me joyful."

"Or even just he'd tell us about saber-toothed tigers."

They walked along, looking down at the stones and fallen trees they had to step over. Clay thought about the giant, who could shake off his blankets of moss and get up to see the whole bright green spring world, deciding instead to try to go back to sleep. The giant had already missed so many centuries, so many eons. Why would he want to miss any more?

Clay suddenly asked Amos, "Do the owl-head people know the rules to baseball?"

Amos turned. "No. It is a game?"

Clay said, "Doesn't matter. There are only three of us anyway, and one of us just grabs the ball in her mouth." He took a baseball out of his pocket. "I don't have any miracles to show you," he said, "but want to play some catch?"

The owl boy looked stiff and anxious. Clay figured he would have to give Amos some tips on how to relax his shoulders before he pitched.

"Yes," said the owl child. "Let's do catch."

CHAPTER NINE

When school ended a week later, the summer stretched in front of Clay like a forest seen from a hilltop: green and unbroken and full of adventures.

Clay wasn't sorry school was over for the year. School during the sickness just felt useless. It just wasn't the same on a screen. Clay wasn't sure he had learned anything at all in the last several months. He missed being in a room with people and making jokes with his friends. So good riddance to school.

If he had not met Elphinore, he would have been miserable—all that summer and no friends to share it with. With her, he never felt alone. Every few days, Amos the Owl Boy would sneak away from the village of the owl-head people, and they would meet up and spend the day walking around in the woods, exploring riverbeds or tossing a ball back and forth.

Occasionally they would go by the Sleepers and say hello to the dismal giant. It turned out his name was Vud. They were trying to convince him to walk around the forest with them. Secretly they wanted to ride on his shoulders. He would just say something rumbly like "Why stand up? I might see what's actually going on in this awful world. The less I know, the better."

Elphinore led them to places they had never seen before: seas of ferns and boulders of pure white marble. She brought them to a clock growing out of a tree, still ticking, but keeping the wrong time. She led them to a waterfall deep in the forest, where the river tumbled down a hillside and split into two—one part of it flowed onward toward the sea, and the other fell into a deep black hole, down into the world below the mountain. There was always a rainbow in the spray. The boys swam by the waterfall while Elphinore stalked around in the shallows, snapping at crayfish. She loved being allowed to share in all their games, running back and forth between them with her tongue lolling out of her mouth, panting with joy.

Clay's parents had started to take Elphinore for granted. Nobody had responded to any of their announcements and advertisements in the *Gerenford Fireside Forum*. The town constable said no one had reported a missing dog of that unusual description—milk white with extraordinary red ears. After a few weeks, Clay's parents stopped talking about finding her home. So without discussion, she stayed.

She proudly ate from her own plastic bowl and was pleased and honored to be allowed to sleep in the boy's bedroom, right beside his bed. After a while, she tried sneaking up to sleep on his bed, sure that she would be sent out to some hidden kennel in disgrace—but instead, he scratched her head and she settled next to him, curled up in a circle, and they were both happy.

Everyone in the family loved Elphinore. Mrs. O'Brian liked her calm presence in the garden; the dog would sit in the shade like a marble sphinx and watch Mrs. O'Brian water the vegetables.

Mr. O'Brian liked coming home from his work on the town's hot, dusty roads and having someone actually happy to see him, jumping up and down. The rest of his family were just trying to avoid one another.

Juniper talked to the dog like she would talk to a doll. She also kept trying to hug her. Elphinore was not crazy about hugs. She backed up, avoiding Juniper's wheeling arms.

The only one who wasn't enthusiastic about the dog was DiRossi. DiRossi didn't really like animals. They all seemed uncontrolled and frightening to her. Even with birds, you couldn't tell what they would do. And DiRossi hated how Elphinore would suddenly start barking her head off at something stupid—a robin on the lawn or a chipmunk on a stump—and it was just so *loud*, so loud and *startling*, and DiRossi would yell, "Arrrr! Shut *up*! Shut *up*, you stupid dog!" Then Clay would say Elphinore wasn't stupid, in fact Elphinore was smarter than DiRossi, and soon everyone would be angry.

So though the members of the family often couldn't stand one another, almost all of them were happy to see Elphinore.

Clay stopped calling his friends as much. When Levi called, Clay was surprised that they didn't have much to say anymore.

"Anything going on?" Clay asked, to make conversation.

"Not really," said Levi, trying to spin a basketball on his finger. It kept wobbling and falling off.

Clay waited for Levi to ask him the same question—if anything was going on—because Clay had a lot to tell him. But instead, Levi said, "Want to hear about me playing *Death Ball 3000*? I did a screenshot of my final score."

Clay made a deal with himself that if Levi asked him "What's up?" he would tell him everything: tell him all about Elphinore, and the owl child, and the wishing lake, and the dismal giant. But Levi didn't ask. He complained a lot about having to mow the lawn.

It's probably better if I don't tell him what's going on, Clay thought. *He'll just be jealous.*

So at the end of the conversation, when Levi hadn't asked him any questions at all, Clay lied, "Yeah, nothing's happening here, either."

Levi said, "Wait. Don't go. I got to tell you about my high score on *Carnival of Blood.*"

And Clay didn't know if by hiding everything that was important to him, he was being kind or being sneaky.

CHAPTER TEN

One day Clay and Amos the Owl Boy borrowed Mr. O'Brian's metal detector from the garage to see if they could find any buried treasure in the ruined tower.

As they walked into the woods with the metal detector, Clay said, "Borrowing isn't stealing if you return a thing."

Amos didn't say anything, which made Clay feel worse.

They walked past the Sleepers and said hello to the dismal giant. Amos bowed to the blue face. "Great Vud," he said, "we of the future greet you."

"You're not from the future," rumbled Vud. "Even worse: you're from the present. This is now."

"Exactly, Vud!" said Clay. "The present is now! You can make the rest of your life whatever you want it to be!"

"Well, that really cheers me up," said Vud. "It moves me right from the pit of despair to the swamp of depression."

Clay rolled his eyes, and the two boys and the dog walked onward to the tower.

All the bushes around the tower were fully in leaf. Clay switched on the metal detector and poked around the blueberries. The metal detector looked like a long pole with a disk on the end. It was made for bigger arms than Clay's; his arm dipped down with the weight as he swung it back and forth.

"My dad uses this at his job," he told Amos. "It helps him find old pipes and stuff when he's doing roadwork."

The detector beeped and squealed when it was above metal. Then Amos and Clay dug. They found part of a metal helmet with holes burned in it. Clay was thrilled. Then he gave Amos a turn with the machine. The owl boy could barely hold the metal detector above the ground, it was so heavy for him. He found some kind of a rusted-out machine with lots of tubes and dials and a gramophone horn, all choked with mud and dirt. Clay said, "It must be from that war you told me about."

Elphinore loved this game. She loved seeing people dig. She could watch people dig all day. Finally, they were doing something that made sense. Sometimes she came to their side and dug with them, hurling dirt out behind her. Then she would lose interest when it wasn't a badger that they uncovered, and she'd go off to pounce on moths.

Clay found a crushed soda can with strange rune writing on it. It had a picture of a fiery horse giving a thumbs-up with its hoof. Amos translated the writing. "'Cavern Cola,'" he said. "'Refreshing as an Underground Lake. Made by Special Appointment of His Majesty the King Under the Mountain.'"

"I wonder what it tasted like," said Clay.

"I have seen underground lakes," said Amos. "They did not strike me as tasty."

Then they found an old key. Clay said, "It looks like the key to an old-fashioned door."

"Old-fashioned?" Amos the Owl Boy said, bewildered.

"Never mind." Clay grinned. "For you, I'm sure this is really modern."

Amos stood up and put his hands on his hips. "I wonder if there is a door somewhere in this tower that leads down to the Kingdom Under the Mountain. It would make sense."

"Yeah! You're right," said Clay enthusiastically. "Because when they were having their war, they would have wanted to get right from their caves up to this tower to defend it."

"It is a shame the tower is so overgrown with green and thorny things. It would be a good adventure to find a forgotten portal to the Kingdom Under the Mountain."

The two poked around in the bushes. They were so intent on looking for a secret passage, they did not notice a dark blue shape winding its way through the underbrush toward them.

"Why is old stuff always buried?" Clay asked. "Is there more dirt now than there was in olden times? If so, does that mean the earth is always getting bigger?"

The elf-hound smelled something approaching—a familiar scent, like hot ceramic. She growled. She barked. Then the scent faded.

The wyrm smiled to herself. The wind was in her favor. The elf-hound could no longer smell her. The wyrm scaled the old broken wall of the tower. She looked down on the two boys, owl head and human. Either head would taste good.

She would follow them and wait for her chance.

The two boys had decided they'd discovered enough scrap metal for one day. They'd come back soon to dig around some more to see if they could discover any other cool stuff or secret passages. Clay was worried about getting the metal detector back in the garage before his dad got home.

They each took one thing that they found: Clay took the remains of the helmet. Amos took the key. They started back toward the human part of the woods, with Elphinore running before them to scout.

The wyrm followed far behind, grinning with her many teeth. She noticed that the elf-hound was usually far in front of the boys—too far to come quickly if the wyrm seized one of them in her teeth and dragged him off to devour.

"Elphinore is like a metal detector," said Clay. "But she discovers adventures. I never would have seen any of this stuff without her." He watched her dart through the trees, leaping cleanly over snags.

"She leads you through the folds between worlds," said Amos. "I wonder if you could still find your way to the Sleepers or the standing stones without her to lead you."

"Yeah." Clay thought about it. "Let's do an experiment!" They were almost at the place where two normal, earthly paths came together at a crossroads. Usually, it was where Elphinore would lead Clay in an unseen fifth direction. "Here's what we can do," said Clay. "You hold on to Elphinore's collar and keep her with you. I'll walk up that path as if I was coming from my house normally. Don't let Elphinore near me. We'll see if I can find the magical path without her!"

So when they reached that spot, Clay left the magic path. He couldn't exactly tell when it happened, but somehow things shifted just slightly. The shadows on the trees were a little different. He was standing on the old normal forest paths he'd walked with his family for years.

He went toward his house ten feet or so, then turned around. He paced toward the crossroads.

Two paths came together: four directions in all. There was nothing that *hid* another path. There were no big bushes there. But he could no longer see Amos or Elphinore.

"Hey! Are you guys still there?"

A voice came from somewhere: "We're standing right here."

"Can you see me?"

"Not from here."

"I can't see you." Something was moving and crackling through the leaves. "Oh, wait! I think I hear you." He walked toward a big, dark fir tree. "I can hear you over here."

"No," said the owl child's voice. "That's not us. You sound like you're moving away."

There was a rustling in the branches of the tree. Clay said, "No, I can hear you."

Amos said, "Brother Clay, that is not us."

"Yeah it is," Clay demanded. "You're right—"

He reached out his arm to point, and then saw the snarling blue head rearing up from the underbrush—he bellowed in surprise.

The wyrm rushed for him.

"Amos! Elphinore!" he yelled, and ran as quick as he could.

The beast hurtled toward him, carried on six squat claws.

"Brother Clay!" the owl child cried, and Elphinore barked crazily in warning and rage. But their voices came from nowhere.

The monster was on him. She flung her great weight at him, claws scratching at the air.

CHAPTER ELEVEN

Clay swung the metal detector right into the leaping serpent. It smacked into her and knocked her sideways—but the neck of the machine snapped. The wyrm landed curled and in pain in the brambles. Clay staggered, tripping over fallen branches. He tried to run. A sharp pain shot up through his ankle. He'd twisted it—but he had to get away. The wyrm let out a raspy growl of anger.

Clay sprinted as hard as he could. At each step, his ankle nipped him. He could hear his two friends stomping back and forth through the dry leaves, but they couldn't find him. He yelled, "This way!"

The monster flipped over and uncurled and darted after him, her head swinging from side to side as she ran. One of her claws was lamed—but that still meant she had four more good legs than Clay.

Desperately, Amos yelled, "Brother Clay?"

"Over here!" Clay yelled back, scrambling over rocks. He flung down the broken metal detector, a mess of snapped plastic and dangling wires. He heard the scritching of the monster's claws as she surged toward him.

Clay stopped short—he had reached the edge of the little waterfall where he had splashed with Amos and the dog. The river tumbled down between boulders into pools and a deep crevasse in the earth. He would have to get across the river to escape from the monster—and he was pretty sure she was better at climbing than him.

One hope: a fallen tree that led across the river. But if Clay fell off it, he'd tumble down through boulders and perhaps into the hole that plunged straight down into the darkness.

Unsteadily, he stepped onto the tree trunk. It was slick and slippery from the spray. It wobbled, balanced uneasily on the rocks. He held his arms out like a circus acrobat. He put one foot in front of the other.

And then the monster behind him lunged.

Its claws scraped across him, and he tumbled into the water.

Splash! For a second, he couldn't see anything. The shock of the cold hit him. He threw his arms out and thumped against rock.

He opened his eyes. He was on the far side of the tree trunk from the waterfall, about neck-deep in the water. The wyrm had slithered out on the trunk and was grinning down at him, jaws open, a claw ready to take off his head.

Clay took two unsteady steps backward. The water roared around him, pushing him toward the beast and the waterfall. The wyrm made a hideous ticking noise with her tongue.

And then he saw a white streak: Elphinore was darting toward them, barking wildly to attract the monster's attention.

The wyrm turned. She hissed at her old enemy. She slashed with her claws. Elphinore dodged, then lunged—ears back, eyes sharp, teeth bared. Clay had never seen her like this before. Frankly, it was terrifying.

Elphinore sank her teeth deep into the monster's neck. But the price was high: the wyrm twisted and clawed and slashed three huge furrows in the dog's hip.

Elphinore rolled and then caught herself, crouched for another attack.

Amos ran up, making a weird, haunting hooting from his beak.

The two magical creatures faced off, perched on the fallen log: the small dog and the huge lizard. Red blood welled up from the white hound's wounds.

Elphinore knew now that she could not win. This wyrm was too old, too smart, too strong. Usually there would be a pack of twenty or so elf-hounds to attack and bring down a monster like this. Elphinore was only one.

But she had a duty. And it was worth giving up her life for this person she loved.

She looked into the old wyrm's eyes. They reflected only hunger and malice.

Elphinore heard the human boy yell something to his owl-head friend. But she did not know what it meant and could not know it was a plan.

She prepared to strike.

She prepared to die.

All at once, Clay grabbed her collar from below—and Amos shoved the log off the rocks, off the waterfall.

Elphinore tumbled sideways into the water on top of Clay.

But more importantly, the wyrm, eyes wide with shock, plunged down the waterfall, her tail still wound around the falling log. She slammed into rocks. And then she hurtled into the dark abyss where the water poured all around her.

Up in the sun, Clay held on to the struggling dog. Both of them were soaked. "It's okay," he said to her. "It's okay, girl. It's okay. I got you." She flung out her paws toward the shore.

Unsteadily, he walked over the slippery rocks to the edge of the river. He lifted the dog into Amos's arms, and they set her down on dry land. Then Amos gave Clay a hand up.

The dog limped over to the waterfall and looked down. There was no sign of the wyrm in the tumult of waters.

As soon as Clay pulled himself out of the frigid river, he could feel the wounds in his side from the monster's claws. He was bleeding badly through his shirt. His whole lower leg was now throbbing with pain from running on his twisted ankle.

Hobbling to sit down on a rock, Clay said, "Thanks, Amos."

"It was your idea," said Amos. "I am grateful you are not dead."

"And this girl." Clay reached out to scratch Elphinore's head.

In his odd, formal voice, Amos said, "I vow she is a very good girl." Elphinore was panting heavily and could not move her hind leg. She had drawn it up from the ground to protect it from more damage. "You are both badly wounded," said Amos.

"Yeah. And I wrecked my dad's metal detector. And they'll never let me come out here again with scratches on me like this. They'll think I was mauled by a bear."

Amos was inspecting Elphinore's leg and side. Blood was staining her milk-white fur and pooling with water on the rocks. Every time she moved, the blood welled up in the wounds. Her panting got quicker.

Amos said, "The dog is bleeding too badly for you to return to your home now. Her death is close."

Clay felt his stomach tighten. "No," he said. "She's okay. She'll be okay." He put his hand on Elphinore's head.

The owl child stared at him, unblinking, like the truth. He said, "She is bleeding to death, Brother Clay."

"No!" Clay shouted.

"Yes," Amos said. He thought for a minute, looking at her wounds. He pointed into the dark woods. "You both must come back with me. To my village. We can heal her."

"You can?"

"Yes. That is what we will do. We will have to risk the anger of the elders." Amos nodded his feathery head. "We will go now. We will ask for help."

Elphinore tried to run ahead where Amos had pointed, but she wasn't even able to walk. Her whole body jolted at each step.

"I think we should pick her up," said Clay. "It looks like she's going to faint."

"Yes," agreed Amos.

The dog sat and looked up at Clay, distressed. Her eyes were filled with a terrible trust.

Clay knelt by her. He took off his shredded sweatshirt and tied it around her to try to stanch the bleeding. Then he picked her up. She yelped in pain as her muscles shifted.

"No," said the owl child. "I will carry her. You are bleeding, too."

Amos was small, and the dog was heavy for him. He tottered under her weight.

"You sure?" said Clay.

"I am sure death is real, and that I want both of you to be well."

Limping and burdened, they headed back into the magical part of the forest. They headed for the village of the owl-head people.

Deep, deep below the earth, the wyrm untangled herself.

Finally, she was back in the caverns under the great mountain. Back where she belonged. She would seek out her young. She would never leave them again.

She slithered onward, intoxicated by the friendly, familiar smells of mildew, fungus, and mold.

Chapter Twelve

Their hike through the woods seemed to take forever. Every step bit at Clay: pain from his ankle, pain from his side. His shorts were soaked on one side with his own blood.

Elphinore was sprawled in Amos the Owl Boy's arms. She was panting in short, gasping breaths. Occasionally, she whimpered in pain. She stared at Clay, waiting for him to help somehow. It broke Clay's heart. The boys could see that she was getting weaker. Clay didn't know how much time she had left.

They passed through dark woods of fir and by the trunks of mighty white pines. Walking through the woods hurting at each step was like walking through a nightmare. Clay didn't know where he was going anymore. He let Amos lead him. He just tried to concentrate on each step forward.

Amos had to set the dog down to rest. She staggered weakly in a circle.

"No!" said Clay. "Don't put her down!"

"I must, briefly," said Amos. "I will take up my burden again in a moment."

Clay wanted to pick her up himself, but he knew he shouldn't.

They continued on their forced march through the magical woods, and at last came to the roofs and the steeple of the owl-head village. The mill wheel turned lazily in the summer river. Owl-head people in bonnets and hats walked up and down the street, running errands.

As the boys approached, a hooting went up all around them. A warning, perhaps. Owl-head people stepped out of the houses and stood on their porches and their stone front stoops. They watched the two boys silently. Clay and Amos staggered up the dusty street, watched by the unspeaking crowd.

It would be nice if they would help carry the dog, Clay thought with irritation.

A woman dressed in a wide black dress and black bonnet stepped forward. As soon as Amos saw her, he stopped and bowed his head. The woman stood before them and said to

Clay, "I am Sister Hesther." She indicated a man at her side. "This is Brother Mordenai. We are the head elders of this village. We would welcome you—"

"Thanks. I'm mainly worried about—"

"—except that you are not welcome." Her beak was sharp and cruel. She said, "Young Amos will be punished for bringing you here."

"Don't," said Clay, who was too tired to be polite. "Please don't. He just wants to save my dog."

"Come with us," said Brother Mordenai.

The owl-head elders led the boys up the street. The owl people watched, their heads all turning together. The elders took the boys into an apothecary house, a simple one-room house with herbs hanging from the ceiling, and many jars and tubs of mysterious liquids on shelves. There was a doctor there, a thin owl-head woman, who gently took the dog from Amos and lay her on a wooden table.

"What was the beast that did this, Young Amos?" she asked, unwinding the bloody sweatshirt and inspecting the wound.

"A wyrm."

The doctor nodded. She said, "The wound is deep." Clay watched while she went to the cabinet and took out a shaker like the one he had stolen several weeks earlier. She shook some of the powder into a cream. Then, clicking and clucking to the dog to soothe her, she spread the goo gently on Elphinore's wounds.

The two elders watched.

Without speaking, the doctor came to Clay's side and lifted his arm. She looked at the scratches. She had kind hands, but Clay was nervous having a beak so close to his side. The doctor spread some of the salve on his side. Then she knelt down and began to press his ankle. He flinched in pain. She watched his face.

As if he were not there, she said to the elders, "The human-head people show everything with their mouths, if you can learn to read them." She kept testing pressure with her thumbs, up and down his leg. "There is not much I can do for this ankle. The growth unguent would cause the skin to harden and his bone to grow bumps and spurs. I will deaden the pain for the human-head boy and put a splint on his ankle, but it must heal by itself."

She busied herself tending to his leg.

After a few minutes, Clay could feel the skin on his side pulling together and scabbing over. The magical powder—what he had called Nature Plus—was casting its spell. He looked over at Elphinore. She had slid half upright, looking back with wonder at her own hindquarters, where pink skin was growing over the deep cuts from the wyrm's claws.

The doctor had tied a splint made of mouse skin and birch bark over Clay's ankle. She stood. "I have done what I can do." She walked to the back of the room and sat on a wooden chair. She stopped moving entirely.

Without a word, Sister Hesther opened the door to the apothecary house. Elphinore struggled to rise. Brother Mordenai lifted the dog down from the table. She hobbled on three legs out the door. She was already looking much better.

The two elders led the boys and the dog up to the top of the street, to the church or meetinghouse. The whole village looked as if it were empty. No one was out anymore.

Inside, the church was hot and stuffy in the summer sun. It was very plain. Three flies circled near the windows.

Clay could tell from the way Amos was standing that they were in big trouble.

"Human-head boy," said Sister Hesther. "You will be led away from this place. You will never try to return here. If you ever come here again, we shall lay a curse upon your house."

Brother Mordenai said, "Young Amos, you will be caned, twenty-five lashes. You cannot leave the village until the autumn harvest."

"But Amos is my friend!" Clay protested.

The two elders swiveled their heads to glare at him. "The human-head people are never our friends for long," said Sister Hesther. "You will betray us."

"You can't punish him like that! He just brought me here because he was trying to save Elphinore's and my lives!"

"His crime was not simply bringing you here," said Brother Mordenai. "His crime was befriending you at all."

Clay was about to protest again, but he saw that it was not helping. The clothes of the owl-head elders were formal and old-fashioned, but their eyes were wild, the eyes of predators who hunted in the night.

"Say farewell to your friend, Young Amos," said Sister Hesther. "You shall not see him again."

Trembling, Amos the Owl Boy put his hand out to Clay. "Goodbye, Brother Clay," he said.

Clay shook it. It felt like something an adult would do—if he were an actual man, not just a boy.

"You're really great," said Clay, and felt like an idiot with those two birds of prey watching him.

Already, he missed his friend. As he was brought out of the meetinghouse, he felt the whole summer falling away, falling apart.

A silent owl-head man with a walking stick led him back through the forest to the paths he knew. Elphinore trotted at Clay's side, perfectly content now that her hip was healing. The three pink stripes from the wyrm's gouges were faint. She had started to grow her fur back around them.

The whole beautiful summer. The enchanted forest. The mysterious mountain. The stupid games they played, jumping off the standing stones. All of it was perfect, and it was going to disappear.

He was going to be stuck back in his house, marooned with his family. And Amos would be caned. Screamed at by those awful faces. There was nothing Clay could do.

The owl-head man pointed silently, and Clay found himself on the path that led back home. Miserably, Clay walked away from his friend Amos forever.

To make matters even worse, it only took a day for his father to notice that the metal detector was gone.

"It's not mine!" said his father. "It's the town's! It's the Gerenford metal detector! Do you realize how much trouble I could get into? And where are we going to get two hundred dollars for another one? And, hey, what did you do to your leg?"

Grounded. Clay was grounded. He was not allowed to walk in the woods until he had paid back his father for the metal detector. And Clay had no job.

The skies were overcast, and the next several days it rained. Clay was stuck inside. The dog was bored. She paced through the rooms like she was dreaming again of adventures, longing to be coursing along through the crystalline woods with the People Under the Mountain. Every morning, when he let her out to pee, she galloped over to the trailhead and looked back at him, expecting him to follow.

Then, when she saw he was hanging back inside the house, she walked back with her tail drooping, as if she were returning to prison.

Everything had gone wrong, and Clay wanted to scream.

CHAPTER THIRTEEN

The summer sizzled in the fields and pastures of Gerenford. Even the cows were too hot. When a car rattled by the O'Brian house, it left a haze of golden dust in the air behind it. There were box fans running day and night in most of the rooms, but they just seemed to push hot air around. Sitting on the sofa or on the easy chairs was like being hugged by a sweaty Muppet.

In this heat, time itself seemed to crawl as slow and sticky as honey. The best way to measure the hours was in the bumping of dumb flies against the windows. In that first year of the virus, even the glorious sentence *"The summer will go on forever!"* seemed awful and gloomy: *"The summer will go on forever . . ."*—like a curse, like a prediction of everything coming to a halt until the end of time.

Being trapped together as a family in the heat made everyone even more cross. Except Juniper.

"DiRossi," said Juniper brightly, "I cleaned up your breakfast stuff for you. So you don't have to do it."

"Stop it!" DiRossi shouted. "Stop cleaning stuff up for me!"

"Really, DiRossi?" said their mom. "You wish she didn't clean your breakfast dishes for you? You really wanted to clean them yourself? What about the ones from yesterday? Or the day before!"

"Yes!" DiRossi said, knowing she sounded ridiculous. "Yes, I want to do as *many dishes as possible.*"

"Look," said Mrs. O'Brian. "We're stuck together. We need to stop fighting. We're going to do something fun. We're all going to sit down together on the porch and play a game."

They played Monopoly. It lasted forever.

As Juniper tidily bought up all the good properties on the Monopoly board and as Clay kept forgetting his turn because he had left the table to throw stuff for the dog, DiRossi fumed. She had a couple of friends who were sixteen and could drive. If it weren't for the stupid sickness all over the world, she would be splashing with her friends at one of the town's ponds, not stuck in this broiling house with box fans roaring everywhere and her little sister following her around all the time trying to make friends with her.

Nobody understood what DiRossi was going through. That was DiRossi's big complaint. Her dad had his job, which kept him busy. Her mom had her garden. Juniper was always happy when the family was together, no matter what they did. And Clay had found that dog. Even though Clay was grounded until eternity, DiRossi still watched jealously as Clay threw the ball to the dog in the yard or whispered things to her when they were sitting on the porch. Clay had a true friend by his side. DiRossi had no idea what Clay's excuse was for looking so miserable all the time.

DiRossi was alone except for online. She and her friends saw each other on their phones and talked about how boring and stupid everything was, or they met in online worlds, where they could vent their frustration by blowing up zombies at beach resorts.

DiRossi decided that no one in her family understood her at all.

She looked down at the Monopoly board. The game was going to go on for another seven hours or something, and Juniper was going to win. And here she was stuck with all of them.

"You're doing really well," Mrs. O'Brian said to Juniper. "Good for you!"

Juniper smiled. "When I win, you can have all my money, DiRossi, if you want it."

This was the last straw. DiRossi stood up. "I don't want your *fake money, Juniper!*" She pounded the table. "It's not real! None of it's real! It's just all of us going around in circles forever in a sports car and a shoe!" She grabbed the edge of the board and dragged it off the table; she flapped the hinged board so colored money filled the air and metal pieces bounced all over the deck.

She enjoyed the shocked looks on Juniper's and Clay's faces.

Then she discovered she was crying. She couldn't explain why. Instead she sobbed, "I wanted Park Place."

She ran inside and up the stairs. She went into her room. Though the fan roared in her window, it was still too hot. She lay down on her bed. Her bed was even hotter. She pulled down all the shades to keep the sun out.

She lay there for a few hours. She wanted everyone to worry about her. They would come upstairs and say, "What's wrong?" and she would tell them, and then maybe her mom would say, "I didn't get it, honey. Of course you can see your friends." Instead of being hyper about infection.

DiRossi did stuff on her phone. She watched videos of fish eating other fish. She watched gossip videos about bands. Everywhere, though, there were people talking about how many people the sickness had killed and how many people were out of work because of it.

There was a soft knock on the door. She didn't answer. If they wanted to know what was wrong, they could ask.

"It's Clay," said Clay.

"Come *in*," said DiRossi.

Clay came in and closed the door behind him. "It's really hot in here."

"I know. It's climate change. Nobody in this family thinks about that but me."

Clay looked uncomfortable in her lair. Good.

He said, "Mom is trying really hard. I know we're all stuck here, but—"

"You don't care if you're stuck here!" DiRossi accused him. "You're leading your perfect dog life with your dog."

"Just," said Clay, "Mom is trying to make things okay for us."

DiRossi stared at him. She hoped it would make him embarrassed and then he would leave. *"And?"* she said, as poisonously as she could.

He admitted, "And she says it's your turn to help with lunch."

DiRossi shrieked at him and pushed her way past him. She wanted to blow up the house with dynamite. She ran out the front door and into the woods.

Even worse, that stupid dog of Clay's followed her, dorky with excitement, leaping up and lunging past her. Elphinore galloped ahead and then stopped on the path, looking back at DiRossi as if she expected DiRossi to jump around and play with her.

The dog hadn't walked in the woods for a couple of weeks, since Clay was grounded. She raced along the path and then returned, tail wagging, drawing DiRossi onward. DiRossi stomped through the forest and hated the fact that her footsteps were so loud in the leaves. Stupid leaves.

DiRossi didn't recognize where she was anymore. She wondered if she could find that weird circle of standing stones.

Elphinore bounded through the forest until they came to a place with many long mounds of earth crowned with trees. In the middle of them, there was a huge blue face sticking out of the ground.

DiRossi assumed it was a statue. She walked over to examine it.

The eyes snapped open and rolled toward her. She stumbled backward in surprise.

"Thank goodness," said the giant. "You're not the boy. I suppose you can't be much worse."

DiRossi narrowed her eyes. "What boy? Is his name Clay?"

"Who learns their names? It might encourage them."

"I'm Clay's sister."

"Ah," said Vud, the giant. "He has not been by for a while. I had assumed he was dead. You little creatures live for such a short time. Or perhaps he *is* dead, and in his last whispered words, he requested that you come and tell me. Spare me nothing. I will shed no tears."

"He's not dead."

"Oh," said Vud. "Better luck next time."

"You don't like Clay?"

"I can't get back to sleep because at any moment, he and his friend might come skipping by and wake me up with their chirpy voices and their singsongy attitudes."

DiRossi wondered who Clay's friend might be.

Elphinore had walked over to the side of the giant's head and was digging gently in his ear.

"Oh, marvelous," said Vud. "This dog woke me from a million-year sleep by rooting around in my nose."

DiRossi was anxious to impress the blue face. "I know! She's so irritating. She's always so happy."

"Don't worry," said the giant. "Soon enough, her joy will be over, and she will rot in the ground." He sighed and then added, "Just like you."

DiRossi said, "What about you?"

"Time is my curse," said the giant. "I plan to spend the rest of my billion-year life mourning for the time that I have already wasted asleep." He sniffed, wrinkling his nose. "Just the thought of all those years I missed makes me want to close my eyes and never wake again. There's no way I can face life now."

DiRossi thought there was a flaw somewhere in this logic, but she couldn't put her finger on it right then. It didn't matter: the giant was a remarkable personality. He was so sour and unhappy that she wanted to impress him. So she said, "I *totally* know what you mean. We're a lot alike."

"I am like no one. I am utterly alone. Trapped in this world."

"Yeah," agreed DiRossi. She sat cross-legged on the fallen leaves. She had finally found someone who understood her.

Later that day, when DiRossi returned from the forest, she seemed a little happier than usual. She even patted Elphinore's head and gave her a treat.

Over the next several days, the family noticed a strange change in DiRossi. She seemed to really look forward to taking Elphinore out for walks. Clay was jealous, but he knew the dog needed exercise. DiRossi would take the dog out into the woods and would be gone for a few hours with her sketch pad and her pencils. When Mrs. O'Brian asked what DiRossi was drawing, she didn't have an answer, but all of her blue pencils were worn down to nubs.

And she was always saying things that sounded like quotes from some famous person, though no one knew who. She would walk into the living room when the family was watching a sitcom and announce to them all, "Laughter is the sound you make when you're trying to hide choking on tears." Then she would walk out.

Or she would say, "The river of time! It flows so fast. The current is without mercy." Or "You never step in the same river twice, because after the first time, you've put your feet in it, so it's all dirty."

When Juniper got on her nerves, DiRossi bent down scarily over her sister and said, "Little child! You are short, and so is your puny human life!"

Of course, she was hearing all these things from the dismal giant. She spent hours curled up by his face, listening to him discuss how everything was getting worse. Apparently, back when he walked the earth, a hundred million years ago, which was long before humankind, things had been really great. Huge forests, giant seas. Then the long silence of the ice. DiRossi wished she could have been alive back then.

Her friends from school were getting tired of her. When they all talked together on their computers, she didn't seem interested in what they had to say. When Kayla mentioned how much fun they had all had together in Mrs. Grotis's class a couple of years before, DiRossi sighed that nothing had been quite as much fun since the arrival of the mammals. When Jed said he had just gone swimming at Walsh Pond, DiRossi said *that* dumb little puddle was nothing compared to swimming with the plesiosaurs and trilobites in the oceans before the great comet fell.

People stopped inviting her on calls.

She didn't care. They were stupid anyway. She dressed in big, shapeless clothes and haunted the woods with Elphinore.

She imagined the day when everyone had gone back to school, and they were sitting there, wondering where she was—and then, outside the windows, they would see a huge, looming blue figure. His head would be as tall as the trees that lined the driveway. And sitting on his shoulder would be

DiRossi. The whole school would run to the windows. They would spill out all the doors and yell questions up to her and the giant in amazement. Even the smartest teachers would be like "What strange and fascinating things has DiRossi seen?"

But DiRossi and the giant would answer no questions. It was no use trying to explain things to a crowd of people shouting in the school parking lot.

Then, with one sad, final glance at their hometown, DiRossi and her giant would head off to the highway, with the giant's blue head bobbing along above the trees. They would wander the globe, curing world hunger, with Vud dragging a giant plow—and then, when they'd fixed that, they would go off and find a cave somewhere in the glaciers up north, where winter was one long dark night. They would have deep conversations by the campfire.

DiRossi couldn't wait each day to get back to Vud and hear him tell her poetic, tragic things about how there was so little time or so much of it. Each morning when it wasn't raining, she would urge the elf-hound to lead her to her dismal friend: "Where's Vud? Can you find Vud?" The dog's face would split in a grin, thrilled to be asked, and she'd lunge off into the forest with DiRossi following close behind.

Vud would be facing away when they arrived. He would

hear them, though, as they crunched across the leaves. He would sigh deeply and say something like "The path leads in two directions, girl. Both of them away from me."

Clay had no idea what was going on. He was stuck going to work with his father. It was part of learning responsibility since he had lost the town's metal detector. His father took him along in the road grader. It was a big machine with what looked like a long razor on it. They drove along the dirt roads of Gerenford, scraping the surfaces so they weren't bumpy. But Clay was getting suspicious that DiRossi had found something cool. Or even worse, something dangerous.

He didn't know how to ask about it without giving away the secrets of the forest.

"Hey, DiRossi," he said. "Have you noticed anything weird in the woods?"

"Weird like what? You? You're here at the house."

"Like a village you've never noticed before. Or a magical tower."

"Oh, brother."

"Or a big blue giant."

"Really? Were you hit on the head?"

"No," said Clay. "Scratched in the side by a kind of flat dragon. But that wasn't because of the giant."

"This is ridiculous," said DiRossi. She turned to leave.

"No," said Clay. "There's a lot of stuff out there that's dangerous. If you ever see an owl-head person, you have got to—"

DiRossi yelled at him, "You don't own those woods, Clay! You don't own everything in them! You act like everything out there is your big secret! And you keep it from the rest of us! Well, some of us have our own secrets, too! Okay?"

She stormed off. Clay heard her calling for Elphinore. Meanwhile, here he was, stuck in the house.

Clay ran down the stairs. "No!" Clay shouted. "You can't take her today. She's staying with me today."

DiRossi wasn't going to be stopped. In a fake excited voice, DiRossi said to Elphinore, "You wanna go for a walk? Wanna go for a walk? Come on! Come on, girl!"

"Don't go, Elphinore!" said Clay. "You stay here with me."

In an even brighter, faker voice, DiRossi said, "Walkie? Walkie, walkie?"

Of course the dog was overjoyed. She heaved into motion and tore across the yard, disappearing up the path. "That's right, girl!" DiRossi called after the dog. It made Clay sick to hear it, and to know that Elphinore was fooled by DiRossi's fake fun act.

He yelled, "She's my dog!"

But DiRossi just blew him a kiss from the edge of the woods and said, "Back in a couple hours!"

"Mom!" Clay screamed.

As he went inside to complain, someone else, though, decided to follow DiRossi. Juniper had heard the whole thing, sitting on the porch with her stuffies. She checked to see if the coast was clear, and then she ran to catch up with her sister.

Her plan was to watch DiRossi and see where she went. Juniper knew she was big enough to keep DiRossi's secrets. She rushed along the path, dreaming of hanging out with her sister at the ring of standing stones—maybe inventing a game where you have to bounce a ball off a different stone each time. Soon, however, she was out of breath.

DiRossi could hear her sister puffing along behind her. Juniper was terrible at hiding.

DiRossi turned around and yelled, "Stop it! Go home!"

She was greeted by a silent wood and one ash tree with a leg in pink shorts.

"I'm warning you," said DiRossi. "Go home."

The ash tree and the person behind it didn't move.

DiRossi stormed ahead along the path. She could not believe that even this—her secret friendship with a buried, unhappy blue giant—was going to be taken away from her.

She wasn't allowed to go *anywhere* without her family and wasn't allowed to do *anything*. Her family was everywhere. All the time. She couldn't stand it.

When she reached Vud, she exclaimed, *"Is there anything worse than sisters?"*

She looked backward to make sure that Juniper heard the answer.

"No," said Vud calmly. "It was one of my sisters who cursed me and the others you see here to ten million years' sleep."

"The really little sisters are the ones you want to step on most, aren't they?"

"For that, I would have to get up."

Juniper had still not appeared on the path. DiRossi was looking forward to her sister being terrified by the giant's face sticking up out of the ground. DiRossi would stand in front of the great Vud and exclaim, "Do you see now, Juniper? There are some things you just don't understand! Visions of a vanished world! A world where wind blew across the endless glaciers for a million years, and everything *died*!"

But Juniper didn't appear.

Maybe she had gotten better at hiding. "Come on out, Juniper," DiRossi ordered.

Nothing.

"Come on, Juniper."

Nobody.

"If she is a mortal," said the giant, "she must follow the dog closely. Otherwise, she will not step sideways into the hidden places."

DiRossi didn't understand, exactly, but now she was worried. Juniper might be lost in the woods. Unable to follow.

"One sec," DiRossi said to the giant, and ran back along the path.

"'One second'? Years pass in seconds," the giant mumbled to himself. "Cities crumble in the time it takes to blink my eyes."

DiRossi called out to Elphinore, "Where's Juniper? Huh, girl? Where's Juniper? Find Juniper! Juniper?"—hoping that by repeating the name enough, she'd remind the elf-hound of her sister.

DiRossi ran a half mile back along the path calling Juniper's name. No one answered. The sky was dark. The woods were silent, as if waiting for a terrible prank.

DiRossi was frantic. She jogged back to her big blue friend. "Vud!" she said. "Vud, my sister disappeared somewhere in the woods!"

"This place is filled with holes in time and space. The happy news," said the giant unhappily, "is that she doubtless appeared in some other woods. In some other world. We might hope it's one with at least some air. And not too many carnivorous trees."

"Come on!" said DiRossi. "Sit up! Please! You can help me look!"

"If she survives the first night, perhaps she will eventually set up a small homestead. A hut. She will grow older in that other world. Maybe one day she will marry a talking cricket and farm aphids with him." The giant cleared his throat. "Just a guess."

"Come *on*, Vud! You can find her in six seconds! You're so tall!"

"Is one tall when one is lying down? No: one is long."

"You know what I mean!"

"It has been ten thousand years since I was tall. Since I stood."

Breathlessly, DiRossi said, *"Then, this is the moment!"* She swished her hands upward.

"The sorrow of this world is too great, child, for us to rise. Instead, we must close our eyes and—"

"You do *not* have to close your eyes! You have to stand up on your stupid, giant feet!"

"Searching, rescuing. These are for better people than me. I am made to lie in the woods, listening to the solemn symphonies of the aspens on my knees."

"Vud! Get up right now! You're my friend!"

At this, for once, Vud was silent.

DiRossi waited. Now he was going to get up. Now he would finally stand. He would allow boulders and dirt and trees to drop off him. He would pick her up in the palm of his hand. He would stride through the wood. They would pass into other worlds if necessary. And DiRossi would point to her sister, who would be crying alone in the dark, tangled forest, with beasts all around her.

No. DiRossi realized: The giant wasn't silent because he was gathering strength to rise. The giant was silent because he was waiting for DiRossi to recognize that he was not her friend, but he didn't want to tell her that to her face. He wanted her to figure it out herself, from his silence.

She glowered at him. He stared, unconcerned, toward the blue sky and waited for her to realize everything he would not say.

The last thing she said to him was "Coward." And then she ran back the way she came, following Elphinore.

DiRossi and the dog jumped along the path, scrambling

up and down slopes and over little creeks. They passed by an overgrown gazebo of stone. They found a marsh where little bridges led over little creeks. They went through dark woods where the spruce and firs smelled sweet.

And they came out by the standing stones.

DiRossi gasped. There was her sister—standing next to a monster.

It was a creature like a child, dressed in brown tweed, but its head was wild-eyed: an owl's.

"Get away from my sister," croaked DiRossi.

"This is Amos," said Juniper.

"Attack!" DiRossi ordered Elphinore.

Instead, the dog went over to the owl-head boy and energetically wagged her tail. He held out his hand, and she licked it.

"Go home, Juniper," said the owl-head boy. "It has been a pleasure to meet you."

"Who are you?" DiRossi demanded.

"He's Amos," Juniper repeated.

The owl boy turned to DiRossi. "Tell your brother that on Midsummer's Eve, the gates to all the worlds will be open. There will be festivities like none he has ever seen."

"You know Clay, too?" DiRossi said.

The owl boy continued, "If he attends that night, he should wear a mask so his face cannot be seen, but have on red trousers so I know him. Some will be masked. No one will know his head is human. I will look for him. Owls have good eyes."

The owl boy bowed to Juniper, and she bowed back. "It was a pleasure meeting you, Juniper Human-Head." He bowed to DiRossi, and she just stared. Then he walked off behind the stones.

"We're going home," said DiRossi. She held out her hand. Juniper reached up and took it, and they walked home together.

That evening, on the screened-in porch, DiRossi whispered the owl boy's message to Clay—about the celebration on Midsummer's Eve, and the mask that should hide Clay's face, and the red trousers that would identify him.

"Did you meet anyone else out there?" he asked, nervously.

"Yeah," DiRossi admitted. "Some dumb giant."

"Vud," Clay confirmed. "He's kind of depressing."

"He's so boring," said DiRossi.

"He seems sort of stuck."

"And he always changes the amount of time he says he's been asleep," DiRossi said. "One million years. Ten million years. Sixty million years." She rolled her eyes.

Clay considered this. "You think he's lying about how long it was?"

"It was probably, like, last January," said DiRossi. "You can never trust what giants say."

They went in to make ice cream sundaes while, out on the dark lawn, lightning bugs flashed like the stars in an ancient, arctic night.

CHAPTER FOURTEEN

Midsummer approached. The town smelled like cow poo from the dairy farms baking in the sun. Clay hadn't been able to see Amos the Owl Boy for more than three weeks.

He didn't actually mind spending the days in the road grader with his dad anymore. He liked the roar of the machinery and the trucks. He liked watching the bumpy road that stretched in front of them turn into a smooth road behind them. He liked his dad explaining things to him about culverts and water bars.

When Clay got home in the afternoons, Elphinore would wag her tail and dance. They'd play games in the yard. She couldn't wait for him to come home.

When she had been one of the royal elf-hounds of the People Under the Mountain, she hadn't been allowed to play games. She had to do what the Master of the Hunt commanded or he would kick her. She and the other dogs of the royal palace always had to be serious and ruthless. They were not supposed to be animals, exactly—they were supposed to be weapons. They were chasing wyrms through crystal forests, or hunting the sacred White Boar that hid on the mountaintop, or baying after the stag that turned into a man and ran between worlds. If Elphinore had ever chased something as small and useless as a squirrel, she would have been punished.

Now she loved chasing squirrels, running after them, bounding across the lawn, and watching them scurry up trees; and she barked, joyfully, just as happy not to catch anything, because the real joy was in making things jump.

Clay wasn't allowed in the woods, so he had to walk her on the road. This was tougher than walking her in the woods because she was hard to control. Elphinore was so excited about everything that she would run into other people's yards and sniff around their barns. She got a hungry look in her eye when she saw chickens.

Clay's parents told him that he would have to walk her on a leash. She couldn't just roam free on the road. When Clay's dad was at the Agway, he bought a new leash and collar for the dog. The old collar, the one with Elphinore's name written in trashy gemstones and mysterious symbols, didn't have any way to attach a leash on it.

Clay's mom and dad talked about it that evening. "Stopped at the Agway," Clay's dad announced. "Got a leash and collar for the dog." He knelt down and unbuckled the old collar. "What'd you do today?"

"I applied to a few jobs," Clay's mom answered. "But no one is hiring. I don't know what we're going to do. We're running out of money, even with you working. How much were the leash and collar?"

"Twenty dollars." Clay's dad snapped the new collar into place around Elphinore's neck. "Here," he said, handing the old bejeweled collar to Mrs. O'Brian. "What do you want to do with this one?"

"It's so heavy and ugly," said Mrs. O'Brian. "It's way too Beverly Hills for a dog in Gerenford." She went over to the kitchen trash can, flipped the lid open, and dropped the collar in. Then she leaned on the counter. "Where are we going to find money? We need money, Barry. Especially having to buy the town a new metal detector. And I wish we could get a new washer since the old one was ruined by cotton trees."

"We'll figure something out, honey," said Mr. O'Brian. He rubbed his wife's cheek. "We always do."

Nobody mentioned to Clay that they'd actually thrown Elphinore's old collar into the trash. A couple of days later, Clay's mom took the trash to the dump. No one in the family noticed.

Clay liked Elphinore's new royal purple collar. It was simple and clean and elegant, just like her. He walked her proudly down the road. Sometimes the neighbors stopped him and asked him what kind of dog she was.

"Bulgarian elf-hound," he said.

One day Mrs. O'Brian found Clay taking all the old newspapers and paper grocery bags out of the recycle pile and sneaking them downstairs. In the basement, he had set up a work space with a big roll of chicken wire from the garden.

"What are you doing?" she asked him.

"Making a mask," he said. "A papier-mâché mask." He dipped strips of newspaper in glue and draped them onto a shape he'd made out of wire.

"A mask of what?"

"A dragon," he said.

"What for?" she asked. "There aren't any costume parties anymore, with the sickness."

Clay didn't meet her eye. He just kept dipping strips of newspaper in the clammy glue. He said, "You never know when you'll need a mask."

It was mid-June. Midsummer was approaching: the ancient celebration of the longest day of the year. A day that people once believed was holy; a night when the gates to other worlds supposedly opened and the spirits walked through the mountains and across the marshes and on the stony shore.

The old-timers of Gerenford, farmers like Levi's grandpa, warned people to stay out of the forest on Midsummer's Eve. No one would go near Mount Norumbega on that night. Too many people had disappeared there on Midsummers past. If you were smart, you stayed at your own farm, lit a bonfire, and maybe grilled hot dogs.

DiRossi knew what Clay was doing. She came down to the basement and stood with her arms crossed. "You're going to meet the owl boy for that magic party in the woods," she said.

"Don't tell Mom and Dad!" he whispered. "Please! I never get to see Amos anymore!"

"I won't tell them," said DiRossi. "If you let me come, too."

"Aw, no," said Clay. "Come on."

"I've been to more parties than you. I can wear a mask. I have red pants."

Clay frowned and thought about it. He was actually a little scared of being on the slopes of Mount Norumbega on Midsummer's Eve alone. He didn't know what weird creatures and sights he would see. It wouldn't be bad to have DiRossi with him. She had experience fighting mushroom people online, at least.

"Okay," he said. "Just, we got to be careful. The owl-head people will be really angry if they find out I'm there."

DiRossi smiled. She actually smiled. "Cool!" she said. "Thanks, Clay!"

"What's everybody doing down here?" said Juniper, hopping down the last steps. "Are you making a diorama of a rock?"

"It's a dragon," said Clay. "A mask. We're talking about masks." He and DiRossi exchanged looks. Neither of them wanted to be responsible for Juniper being in the woods in the middle of the night when the gates between the worlds were open.

Juniper said, "Are you both making masks? I want to make one, too."

DiRossi said, "I already have a mask. An old-fashioned white mask like they used to wear in Italy at carnivals."

Juniper stared in both their eyes. She said, "You're getting ready to go to the owl-head boy's party."

"No," said DiRossi. "I'm not invited."

"I want to go," said Juniper. "I'll make a mask."

Clay and DiRossi exchanged a look. The look said: *Trick her.*

"Okay," said Clay. "Make a mask. We'll tell you when the right night comes."

"Hooray!" said Juniper. She rushed up the stairs and began doing something disastrous with cardboard and scissors.

"I feel bad, lying to her," said Clay, "but it's too dangerous. We just won't tell her when Midsummer comes."

Juniper yelled down, "Sparkles! Sparkles, sparkles, sparkles! I want my mask to be sparkly!"

"We can't let her go," DiRossi agreed. "Mom would triple kill us."

By the afternoon of Midsummer's Eve, Clay's dragon mask was finished. He had painted it. It was red, to go with his red pants. He never normally would have worn red pants without complaining. They were his Christmas pants. They were a little too small for him.

He couldn't wait to wear them. He couldn't wait to slip through the forest in his mask, meet his owl-head friend again, and see more wonders.

The minutes ticked down. That evening, the family ate dinner. Clay and DiRossi couldn't help smiling secretly at each other in excitement. Juniper didn't suspect anything.

Clay pretended to go to sleep. He could barely stop himself from wriggling around with excitement. He waited for Juniper's breathing to grow slow and regular. She slept with her cardboard mask under her pillow.

At around ten thirty, Clay got up. Elphinore shook herself and wagged her tail slowly. She sensed adventure.

The party between the worlds was about to begin.

Chapter Fifteen

Three figures slipped across the yard from the O'Brians' house to the trail. One had the head of a dragon. The other had a pale white face like porcelain in a dark hoodie. They both wore pants of red. Before them ran an elf-hound, thrilled to be racing toward the unknown.

The woods that night smelled sweetly of warm grass, and blossoms, and wild mint in the pastures. Clay and DiRossi scrambled along the path, both holding flashlights. They hardly needed them, though: the moon was so bright above the trees that everything was lit up blue. Throughout the woods, like the windows of a hidden city, fireflies were flashing.

"It's okay to lie to Juniper, right?" whispered Clay. (Even though they were too far from the house to be heard, it felt like a night when you should whisper.)

"Yeah," said DiRossi. "She'll be safer at home. Turn off your light."

Something was coming along a nearby path.

The two kids shut off their flashlights and stepped sideways into the bushes. They saw a tall being wrapped in a white sheet; it had a head as large and strange as a cow skull. It carried a staff with a small birdhouse on the end, and from the round door of the birdhouse came light.

Elphinore was still on the path, and she growled.

The creature said, "Peace, elf-hound," and held out its claw for sniffing. It passed along and disappeared into the woods.

Clay and DiRossi stared at each other in shock. Clay adjusted his dragon head. It had slipped, and he could barely see out the eyeholes. They waited for a while before they continued. They didn't want to catch up to the creature.

The dog led them through the woods toward the standing stones and the great Sleepers. Now the three of them could see other guests pacing through the forests: strange beasts usually hidden from the eyes of human-head people. Some were tall and some were tiny. They were all dressed in their party best. The fireflies lit the way for them.

DiRossi and Clay stood up very straight and walked like they, too, were creatures of another world and belonged at the party. They were glad they wore masks. A few of the beings around them were masked, too—though the faces beneath those masks would clearly be stranger than anything ever seen on Halloween.

Brother and sister followed the other guests toward music and light. They passed by the wishing lake, where little boats with lanterns passed to and fro. They came to the Sleepers, where crowds had gathered and were standing in the groves on top of the slumbering giants. A fish-head band in armor, with great bristling spines on their backs, played welcoming fanfares. They blew on trumpets with their mouths and on pipes with their gills.

"Oh," said DiRossi, "Vud must hate all this noise." She ran through the crowds of creatures to the side of Vud's face. Elphinore ran up the giant's lip and licked the tip of his huge nose.

"Superb," said the blue giant miserably. "Something to make the evening worse."

DiRossi said, "Vud! It's really me! And Clay!"

"I know," said the giant funereally. "That's why I was so unexcited."

"Does all this noise bug you?" Clay asked.

"No, I love watching people have more fun than me," he said. "Nothing better than lying here, depressed, not able to move my arms, with creatures around me rejoicing, dancing, and falling in love on my stomach."

"We could stuff your ears," said DiRossi. "Maybe it would be quieter."

So Clay and DiRossi gathered dirt and leaves by the armful and shoved them into the giant's ear holes until they were absolutely plugged.

"Is that better?" DiRossi shouted at him.

"I can't hear you," said the giant, unhappily.

Together, brother and sister shouted, *"IS THAT BETTER?"*

"Oh," groaned the giant, "now I'll miss everything. The whole party." He closed his eyes and ignored some small many-legged beasts with glass helmets who were staking out a spot on Vud's shoulder to light off fireworks.

The meadow above the owl-head village had been mowed to make a dancing ground. Along one side, long tables were covered with white tablecloths and set up with foods Clay and DiRossi had never imagined: the roasts of beasts who'd never seen the light of day; noodle dishes with bright flowers; green beans that swayed in time to the music.

The music was played by an orchestra on living harps and cranked, bubbling machines and ox-bone viols.

When Clay and DiRossi arrived, the owl-head people and a race of people with horns and the spotted legs of fauns were having a dance-off. The faun people whirled wildly, leaping over each other, spinning out of control, their mouths hanging open. The owl-head people danced severely, in long lines, swinging their arms in unison.

"Those are the owl-head people," Clay explained. "Amos should be around here somewhere." He looked around anxiously for his friend.

Elphinore ran back and forth across the field, sniffing everything. Creatures crowed as they saw her excitement, and they reached out their claws to scritch-scratch her head. She growled at the shirt-o-saurus, who, with the sweater-sheep, was secretly eating off of someone's plate on the grass.

An owl-head boy—much taller and broader than Amos—was walking toward Clay and DiRossi with purpose. Clay shrank back. He knew there would be a terrible price to pay if he was discovered there.

But the owl-head boy walked past Clay to DiRossi. He demanded, "What kind of thing are you under that mask?"

DiRossi shuffled from foot to foot. Finally she said, "Hideous."

The owl-head boy nodded. "I'm Mosef. Do you want to dance?" He offered her his arm.

Soon she was dancing away in a long line of kids—owl-head and otherwise—learning the steps to the adults' dance, laughing and kicking out their legs.

Clay stood alone by the food. He watched them all having a good time.

A squirrel was sitting on the table by the mixed nuts, taking a break to smoke a cigarette.

"That's a bad habit," said Clay. "It will kill you."

"You know what will kill me?" the squirrel said. "Being chased by your dog every time I go out to get my mail."

Clay hadn't thought of that. "Oh," he said. "I'm really sorry."

"Eh," said the squirrel. "Crack me open some of those walnuts and we'll call it even."

Dutifully, Clay began to shell walnuts for the squirrel. Soon there was quite a pile on the tablecloth.

Then a hand grabbed him. "NO!" someone shouted, and shoved him.

Clay stumbled and tripped, falling backward into the grass. His first instinct was panic: he had been found.

But it was Amos himself. *"Don't eat any of it!"* he said.

"Ow," said Clay, brushing himself off and standing up. He righted his dragon head, which was drooping. "I wasn't, Amos. I was cracking walnuts for the squirrel."

"Any mortal who eats the food at this feast will never be able to leave. You will be taken under the mountain for the rest of time."

"Nice to see you, too, Amos," said Clay, with a little sarcasm.

Amos bowed. "It is nice to see you, Clay Human-Head. Your sister told me where you were. I thought she was you, because of the pants."

"This is an amazing party," said Clay. "Where are all these creatures from?"

"They always live around us. But we cannot always see one another. Whenever I am bored, I remember that the world is full of these wonders."

"So what do we do now?"

Amos grabbed his wrist. "Come and let's look into other worlds."

The two friends and Elphinore ran through the woods. They dodged through the ribs and thick black trunks of the white pines. Lovers sat in the trees, holding three hands. Families with insect eyes walked past licking ice cream.

Sometimes they caught sight of Mount Norumbega above the trees. There were fires burning on the heights, and glowing lights drifted up and down over the peak. Clay imagined the people he knew at farms around town sitting on their porches or peeking out their windows and seeing the supernatural glow on the mountain. Clay was proud to be out in the middle of the magical night, the shortest night, the night of secrets.

They came to the circle of standing stones. "There," said Amos the Owl Boy. He fixed his bright yellow eyes on the ring of stones. "I can barely stand to look at it," he said.

At first, Clay didn't understand what his friend meant. But when he stared, he felt as if someone had smashed a kaleidoscope on his head.

The world split around the standing stones. There were routes and aisles to other places there, directions that should not exist. For a second, the two friends just tried to get their bearings.

Elphinore ran ahead, kicking out her legs happily. She grinned back at them, darted into a sunlit canyon—Clay shouted her name, panicked—and then she jumped right back out of a forest of blue ooze.

"Come along!" said Amos, and he jogged toward the gateways to other worlds.

Clay had never had such a good time as that night. He held on to the back of Amos's jacket so the owl boy could peer over a cliff into a cold, steaming sea and watch monsters sun their bellies. They wandered through the ruins of some great city and played hide-and-go-seek among the giant heads of broken statues. Elphinore ruined the game, because she couldn't stop running back and forth between them, wagging, giving away their hiding places. So they played fetch with her between the worlds, hurling a stick into impossible spaces. Her footing was always sure, even when she had to run along a ceiling or through a wall to fetch.

They played tug-of-war between the worlds, with a fir branch disappearing halfway between them.

Then they found a bunch of other kids—mostly owl-head friends of Amos's, but also kids with shells and kids with snouts—and Clay took out his Super Ball, and they spent an hour bouncing the Super Ball into different universes while Elphinore capered between them. She disappeared and reappeared with the ball in her jaws. Everyone clapped and chased her.

Amos pointed out the celebrities he knew. There was the Duchess of the Lake of Wishes dressed in blue velvet; next to her was her consort, the spirit of the River of Time and

Shadow, a woman clad in a sheath of pond weed. There was a family of boulder trolls who lived up near the top of the mountain and rarely came down. People were hanging their coats from a huge dead tree, and among them was a great jelly-like thing from beyond the edge of space, bowing and bubbling to other guests.

Then Amos pointed out a figure with smooth, mirrored skin riding a horse, seated backward. As the horse stalked forward, light struck it, and Clay could see its skeleton beneath its transparent flesh. People bowed to the dazzling rider and backed away.

"Who's that?" Clay asked.

Amos answered, "That is Death, on his pale horse, Trigger Mortis."

The mirrored figure held a long wand with a metal symbol at its tip. It rode past Clay and Amos, who hid behind rocks. It rode up behind a hairy man-creature who was dancing wildly on hooves. Death reached out its wand and touched the man-creature, and the man-creature stopped and looked around. His friends all looked on in horror. The man-creature saw who had touched him. He nodded at Death. He went and hugged another creature, perhaps a creature he loved, and then walked away into the night. The party was over for him.

Death moved along, facing backward on his horse, seeking out his next victim.

"People know that Death is going to be here, but they still come?" Clay said.

"Death is always invited," said Amos. "When he calls, we must go. But knowing that the night may be cut short is what makes it so sweet. It is the reason we must dance."

They went back to their ball game. Clay now kept his eye out for the mirrored figure while still trying to watch the ball ricochet in six directions at once.

DiRossi, meanwhile, was dancing with Mosef and his friends—pretty owl-head girls in calico dresses.

"What kind of a creature are you?" Mosef asked as they do-si-doed past each other.

"A really amazing one," said DiRossi, "but very evil." She figured she didn't really have anything to lose.

Now all the creatures on the dancing green were joining hands. DiRossi held hers out for Mosef to take; on her other side was an owl-head girl named Sharloss. In a long line that stretched half a mile, they danced through the dark woods, all the creatures with their many eyes and antlers and beaks and banners. "Where are we going?" DiRossi shouted at Mosef over the music.

"Everywhere!" he shouted back, and tugged her arm. She tugged back and he almost tripped and they both laughed.

They came to the standing stones and saw all the gates to all the worlds standing open and gleaming. DiRossi saw Elphinore, Clay, and Amos the Owl Boy leaping around with other kids in some ball game.

And then everyone formed a huge circle and began to rotate through the worlds. It was a great dance of time and space. With one step, you would be in a desert, and with the next, in a swamp where great arched necks rose around you. DiRossi had to hold on tight to Sharloss and Mosef, because she didn't want the ring of people to break and find herself flung out alone into one of the weird landscapes. The three of them gripped one another's hands and screamed like they were on a carnival ride.

Through icy nights and mornings on fire, through cities of light, they danced, each following the next in a great ring like Saturn's— and DiRossi laughed so hard with happiness, she couldn't believe she had ever sat in the dark in her room when there were so many directions to look in, so much that was unknown.

I always want to live my life like this, she thought. *Even tomorrow when everything's normal and people have the heads of people.*

She grinned as she passed Clay. He was standing, holding a piece of rope on top of the granite head of a fallen emperor.

He couldn't see that she grinned, because she wore a white porcelain mask and he wore the face of a red paper dragon.

Then she was back in the woods—they were all back in the woods—with the fireflies bobbing around them.

And a nearby hill was rising up on pillars. All its trees were lifted up atop it. Light spilled out from within it. Everyone in the great circle stopped dancing to applaud. They stood on the moss and soft grasses and watched the cap of the hill rise.

Out of the hill poured the court of the Kingdom Under the Mountain. They had come to pay their respects. They wore white bow ties and gloves and black jackets and crowns of leaves and flowers; they wore short, sequined party dresses, and some of the women had peacock feathers in their hair. The Queen Under the Mountain was among them, wearing a tall tiara of icy diamonds and a silver eye mask over her dead white face. She smiled and blew kisses.

And then the Royal Hunt came forth from the hill in red jackets with brass buttons. They rode on proud horses. And they had their elf-hounds pacing at their sides.

Clay was standing in the middle of the ball game, open-mouthed. He hadn't thought about the People Under the Mountain. Of course they were going to be there.

He looked around for Elphinore.

She wasn't there.

"Amos!" he said. "Amos! We got to find Elphinore!"

Amos hesitated, the Super Ball in his hand.

Clay said, "They'll take her!"

Amos said, "She must make her own choice."

Clay didn't like Amos saying that, but it wasn't a time to argue. He said, "She won't be making her own choice if they see her first and grab her and drag her underground." He pulled Amos along. They ran side by side, looking desperately through the crowd.

But Elphinore had already heard the barking of her own elf pack. She was racing toward them as quickly as she could, leaping around deer legs in patent-leather shoes and through the loops of serpent-women. She heard her brother, her sister, her father, all barking proudly to announce the arrival of the Royal Hunt at the party.

For the moment, she didn't even think of the boy who searched the crowd for her. She thought only about the kennel in the cave, the scent of her sisters asleep, the hunts by gem light.

Clay saw her darting toward the elfin troop with their pack of hounds. "Elphinore!" he screamed, anguished. He just had to catch her attention. That was all: If she remembered him, she wouldn't go away. She'd come back to him.

Elphinore skidded to a stop in front of Greykin, the leader of the pack. She panted with excitement. She walked forward to touch noses with him, to remind him of her scent.

He knew her. He growled, and with one quick paw and a snap of his jaws, he threw her to the ground. How dare she come back to them smelling of humans and their dirty world? She quivered on her back.

"Stop it!" yelled Clay, and he rushed out of the crowd to save his dog.

The Master of the Hunt was already there. In his fluting elfin language, he called out to the Hunt that this was Elphinore, the missing dog.

"Elphinore!" Clay cried out, running toward her.

Several guards armed with pikes stepped between him and the dogs.

Elphinore looked up out of the corner of her eye. She saw Clay. She was lying crouched on the ground, expressing her guilt and sorrow. The older dog, Greykin, towered over her.

"Come back with me!" Clay said, almost a sob. "Elphinore!"

The dogs were all around her. She could not remember

where she was supposed to be. She remembered a house where she was allowed to sleep on a bed, and a royal kennel of stone with a velvet cushion just for her. She looked from the dog pack to the boy.

Clay could not get any closer to her. The squires stood in the way. He held out his hand, but it was much too far away for her to sniff.

The Master of the Hunt walked over to her and waved his leather riding crop. She cowered. She remembered what it felt like to be hit with it when she disobeyed.

Helplessly, Clay watched the Master of the Hunt yell at Elphinore. He watched the Master of the Hunt lash out with his boot and kick his beloved dog hard in the ribs. She yelped in pain.

The Master of the Hunt yelled another order at her.

She rose up and, tail curled between her legs, stared at Clay a final time. The other dogs were all around her.

She was going home.

Clay screamed at them all—all the awful People Under the Mountain in their fancy clothes. The Queen herself. The elfin guards frowned. They shoved him backward. He hit the dirt hard. His dragon head fell off. He heard a gasp go up all around as people saw his human face.

The Master of the Hunt unwound a piece of rope and tied it around Elphinore's neck. He handed it to a page boy and pointed back to the hill they had all come out of. The page boy and several guards started dragging the dog away.

She turned her head toward Clay. He could see how frightened her eyes were by how much of them was white.

He could tell she was looking for him, but he could not tell if she saw him.

Then Elphinore, his beloved elf dog from under the mountain, was gone, and the music rose again, and all around the crying boy, monsters danced.

Chapter Sixteen

DiRossi and the owl-head people, along with all the other guests, had watched all this happen. DiRossi was desperate to get to Clay. "Where did my brother go?" she asked Mosef, rising up on her tiptoes to see over the crests and hats and crowns of guests.

"Who is your brother?"

"That kid with the dragon head and red pants."

"The one with the dog?"

"Clay."

Mosef and Sharloss backed away. Mosef drew one arm up in front of him as if it were broken. He said, "Your brother is the human-head person who came to our village!"

"Yeah," DiRossi agreed, without thinking about it. She leaned over to see around some young witches.

"He has been forbidden!" said Mosef. "The elders will curse him!"

"Don't bother," said DiRossi. "Those elf people took his dog. He's never going to be happy again anyway." She craned her neck. She said, "Look, I'm going to see if he's headed home. He must be really upset. Can you check to see if he's up on the dancing green? And if he's there, tell him I'm looking for him?"

Mosef nodded stiffly. "We will," he said. "The People Under the Mountain will punish him greatly for stealing their hound."

DiRossi stared at her new owl friend through her mask. She'd had a great time dancing with them, but suddenly she was aware of how stiff and formal they all were. It made her feel tired. "That's all you've got to say?"

Mosef looked uncomfortable.

DiRossi said, "So I had a really good time hanging with you guys, and I'm not afraid to say it." When Mosef still said nothing, DiRossi took a big breath and said, "I don't care if you say anything or not. We had a good time. Bye."

She ran off into the crowd and left them behind.

She was worried about Clay and Elphinore and a little angry at her new owl-head friends, who apparently weren't such good friends after all. She ran along the path calling out, "Clay!" Creatures were all staring at her.

Then something changed, and there were no creatures anymore. The woods were dark. There were no fantasy lights in the trees.

DiRossi turned on her flashlight. She recognized where she was. She was surprisingly close to home. She realized that she must have stepped right out of the magical wood and into the normal wood. Without Elphinore to guide her, she wouldn't be able to find her way back to the party between the worlds.

She kept on calling her brother's name as she walked toward home.

Something was running along the path toward her.

"Clay?" she said.

She swung her light around. It picked out a milk-white elf-hound with extraordinary red ears.

"Elphinore!" DiRossi said, relieved. She held out her hand. "Hey, girl! Can you help me find Clay? Where's Clay? Where's Clay?"

But that dog was too big to be Elphinore. DiRossi froze. The elf-hound watched her. Then, staring straight into her eyes, he started barking at the top of his lungs.

And the hunt was on. She heard the baying of the pack in the distance.

What were they hunting?

Then she realized: *Me. They're after me.* She ran.

No, she thought, *they're after Clay. But they must think I'm him.* A human in a mask and red pants, running back along a path that smelled of Elphinore.

The sound of barking came from all directions. They were closing in on her.

She burst out of the woods and crossed her family's lawn. The motion-detector light snapped on. Every bush and pebble had its shadow. White dogs poured out of the woods, chased by their own dark shapes. Behind them, someone was sounding hunting horns.

She threw her mask at the lead dog. It bounced off his snout and he stumbled, snapping angrily at the air.

She was at the front door. She ran inside and slammed it—locked it. Safe!

But then she remembered Clay. He was probably still out there.

Her father and mother were up, rushing out of their bedroom. They turned on lights and shouted, "What's going on?" "What's happening?"

"Dogs!" said DiRossi, hoping no one would ask any more questions.

Juniper was coming down the stairs, clutching her cardboard mask to her chest. "Where's Elphy?" she asked. "Where's Clay? They're not in our room!"

Mr. and Mrs. O'Brian were in their bathrobes. They scurried around, looking out windows.

"Who's *that*?" Mr. O'Brian said, horrified.

Out the window, they saw some duke dressed in a red coat and a black hat and armed with a long spear. He was staring in at them. Others were arriving behind him. The yard swarmed with barking dogs.

Mrs. O'Brian was already on the phone to the village police. "Hi, Lucille. It's me. We're under attack by wild dogs and some nutjobs on horses dressed for . . . I don't know what they're dressed for. Olden times?"

"A party back in the day?" guessed Mr. O'Brian.

"A party later than olden times but before back in the day," said Mrs. O'Brian. "Yeah. Of course we're going to stay inside. Thanks. Right. See you."

She hung up. "Where's your brother?" she asked Juniper and DiRossi.

Juniper had started crying. The hunting dogs were leaping at the front door and slashing at it with their claws.

DiRossi said, "Beats me."

Mr. O'Brian came and put his arm around Juniper. "Don't worry, sweetie," he said. "We're safe as long as we're inside."

"Really?" She sniffled.

"Yes, really," he said, and tried to smile.

And then the People Under the Mountain rode through the walls.

To be exact, their horses charged through the house as if the walls did not even exist. The wallpaper, however, did exist, and they burst through it, leaving it torn and hanging. The riders stormed around the family, shouting out threats in a harsh and strange language. They galloped across the sofa, knocking it to pieces. They swung their spears around, and everything crashed and toppled. One rode his horse galumphing up the steps. The carpet tore. The banister on the stairs collapsed.

Another knight jumped through the wall as if it weren't there—but the copper wires running through the wall did exist, and they caught him and burned him. They left stripes on his shoulder. He screamed with anger and began to swing

his sword around, smashing everything in the kitchen. The horse wheeled on its hind legs, coming down again and again to break all the tiles on the kitchen floor.

There was nothing the family could do—four people, three of them in their pajamas, without any way to defend themselves, surrounded by men and women with spears and swords. The O'Brians huddled together, watching everything they owned get destroyed.

Juniper could not stand the chaos. She needed everything to be in its place. She wailed and wailed, shutting her eyes as tight as she could, trying not to see all their things broken and lying damaged on the floor. She hated the magical people for ruining everything.

"Where's Clay?" Mrs. O'Brian demanded. She reached out and grabbed DiRossi and shouted into her face, *"DiRossi! Tell me where Clay is! Is Clay safe?"*

DiRossi couldn't answer. Knights bashed apart the TV screen and the dining room table. They yelled insults at the family in their language, sneering as they destroyed the living room.

Then someone dressed as a duke or a lord called out an order, and hunting horns sounded. The duke pointed back toward the forest.

Suddenly, the Royal Hunt was all business again. They all turned their horses to the north. The duke said a word; the squires blew on their hunting horns. At the signal, the whole Hunt galloped off through the solid walls and disappeared into the woods.

The sound of their horns and the barking of dogs faded.

"The walls," said Mr. O'Brian, looking astounded around his living room. "How did they get through the walls?"

Everything the O'Brians owned was trampled and torn apart. The house was silent. There were hoofprints on the chairs and horse poo on the rugs.

Far off, a single siren sounded. It was the town's one cop car, coming to the rescue.

Juniper leaned into her father and cried. Her mother asked DiRossi again, "Where's Clay? What have you two been doing?"

DiRossi did not know how to answer.

CHAPTER SEVENTEEN

Clay and Amos the Owl Boy were hiding in the shadows as the party went on. Clay was inspecting the hill raised up on pillars.

"We've got to get down under the mountain," Clay said. "We can save her."

"She doesn't want to be saved," said Amos. "She chose to be with the Royal Hunt, Clay Human-Head."

"No, she didn't," said Clay. "She just got excited when she saw them, and she wanted to say hi. She didn't know they'd be mean to her. When they dragged her underground, she was looking for me. She wants me to come find her."

"That is a story you tell yourself to feel better," said Amos.

Clay was suddenly furious with Amos. He said, "Shut up."

"I am only saying the truth."

"Shut up! No, you're not. I'm going down alone if you won't go with me."

The owl child pointed at the hill that was lifted up. Between each set of pillars was a guard with a pike. "You will never get past those guards."

"Why do you have to be like that?" Clay shouted. "You like showing off miracles and marvels when they're things you're used to—but you're chicken when it's anything new."

He stomped off. He shoved his dragon head back on his own head. It didn't matter much whether he disguised himself or not: everyone at the party had seen him and had watched him lose his dog.

"Brother Clay!" said Amos, running after him.

"Don't call me brother anything."

"There are other ways into the Kingdom Under the Mountain."

Clay stopped. "Like what?"

Amos fished around in his pockets. He brought out the rusty key. "The key we found in the tower. We never went back to search for the door it opened."

Clay thought this through, watching the party continue behind the owl boy.

He said, "You're right."

"We could look for the door now."

Clay nodded. "Thanks, Amos," he said, and Amos nodded back.

They ran down the path that led from the standing stones to the tower. The last time they had been there was the day when they had been attacked by the glittering blue wyrm—when Clay broke the metal detector—the day when they were forbidden to see each other again. They had planned to return and look for a door there, but they hadn't seen each other since.

Now, finally, they were at the ruined tower again. It loomed in the dark. Clay turned on his flashlight.

Amos covered his eyes with his arm. "No, Brother Clay," he said. "I will see better without the light."

"Okay," said Clay. "You search that side, I'll search this side." On their hands and knees, they started to scrape away leaves and dirt.

"I am not a coward," said the owl child as they searched.

"I didn't say you were a coward."

"You said I was a chicken. That is not a kind thing to say to an owl-headed person."

"You said my dog didn't like me. That's not a kind thing to say to any kind of person. And it's not true." He turned around to see if the owl-head boy would argue—but for once, Amos was smart enough to keep silent.

They both dug through bushes and ran their hands across the cold stone walls of the tower. It felt so strange to be on an adventure without Elphinore cheerfully bounding back and forth between them, sniffing out chipmunks. Clay hoped she was okay. He hoped she was not scared. He hated the memory of her shocked eyes, her tucked tail. She had protected him; he was supposed to protect her, too. That's what she expected.

But now maybe he couldn't protect her. She had been dragged someplace he could never reach.

The night had turned blustery. The treetops blew back and forth restlessly, as if they were unhappy at the meeting of the worlds. The crickets had stopped singing.

At one point, a magical procession went by. They were beasts dressed in long green robes, with crowns of flowers on their heads. They carried torches and walked in two straight lines, chanting some old song from the beginning of time. Eight of them carried a giant moon that glowed with its own light. They could see the shadow of something moving inside the moon, like a chick in an egg, waiting to be born.

The procession disappeared toward the Lake of Wishes.

The boys held their breath until the solemn parade had passed by. Then they started to search the ruin again. "There must have been a door somewhere in the tower," said Clay.

"Brother Clay!" said Amos. "It is here! Here it is!" He lashed out with his leg at some spiky berry bushes and trampled them to the side. There was an old hatch made of metal set right into the wall of the tower.

Clay rushed to Amos's side. Amos had the key in his hand. He slipped it into the metal lock. It fit. "We must both hold it," Amos said. "The luck will be better."

Clay and Amos turned the key together.

The locked was rusted and wouldn't move. They jiggled the key. Something rattled. Carefully, they tried again. With a nasty-sounding scrape, the key turned in the lock.

The hatch popped open. Cold, underground air tumbled out into the warm summer night.

A set of old stone steps led down into darkness. "The Kingdom Under the Mountain," said Clay in awe.

Amos grabbed him. "You will be killed if you go down there. They will see that you are a stranger. A human-head person."

"Then we need a plan."

"They would kill me, too."

"Unless," said Clay, "they thought we were even stranger than an owl-head person and a human-head person. Your elders could speak their language. Can you?"

"I am no scholar," said Amos. "I know a few words, but only the words a tourist might use."

"That," said Clay, poking his friend in the chest, "is perfect."

He explained his plan.

First, they ran back to the tree where the coats were hung. While Amos kept watch, complaining the whole time—"This is a terrible idea, Brother Clay"—Clay searched through the coats. He swung them aside and measured them all with his eye. Finally, he found one that was just the kind of thing he was looking for: a long coat of silver brocade. He rolled it up and stuck it under his arm.

"Got it," he said, and headed back to the tower.

"Brother Clay, are you sure the dog is worth this danger?"

Clay stopped and glowered at Amos. "You've met her," he said. "What do you think?"

The owl child nodded.

They got back to the tower. The treetops bashed back and forth in the wind. From afar, carried on the wind, there were sudden voices and pieces of music.

"Let's go," said Clay, and he stepped through the hatch.

It was musty on the old staircase. They had to use Clay's flashlight: owl eyes couldn't see in the pitch-dark.

They went down and down and down. As Clay crept down the echoing staircase through cold and murk, he remembered scenes of Elphinore's happiness: the games she made up with sticks, the curl of her sleeping body on his bed, the slow wag of her tail in the morning. When he fed her, she gobbled her food down fast because she couldn't wait to get back to playing, to living. Clay didn't want to cry. The stairs kept twisting down through the darkness, through gloom and chill.

When they thought it wasn't possible to go down any longer, they saw a gleam of light below them. Clay shut off his flashlight, and they began to move more carefully.

The staircase ended, and there was an archway, and through that archway was a faint bluish light. Carefully, they crept forward and peered out.

What they saw underground took their breath away.

Chapter Eighteen

Amos and Clay stared out into the heart of an underground palace. The castle towers were so high that several went right into the roof of the cavern. The whole cavern was lit softly by some kind of artificial sun—a gemstone stuck in the ceiling. Somewhere in this palace, hidden in a maze of chambers and courtyards, was Elphinore.

There were sounds on all sides of the Midsummer celebrations among the People Under the Mountain. The palace courtyard, however, was almost empty. The Queen and her friends were up above, Clay figured, showing off in front of the peoples of the forest.

Clay felt weird, being so far beneath Mount Norumbega. He had been living all his life above this secret city. His little house and his quiet, boring days all went on like normal, and down here, there were miracles.

"Time to make ourselves into a tourist," he said to Amos. He bent down on one knee.

Amos carefully climbed onto Clay's shoulders. Clay steadied himself against the wall and stood with Amos wavering above him. Then Clay unrolled the silver coat. It had four arms. Clay handed it up to his owl-headed friend. And he handed up his papier-mâché mask.

A few minutes later, a group of elfin partygoers walked by, talking loudly and pointing at the thin towers of the palace. Right behind them rose up a weird beast with four arms and a sloppy dragon head.

It was a night where the worlds met. The partygoers didn't take much notice of a strange guest. If it had been a human- or an owl-head person, they would have called for guards. But this was some strange, messy being from a world farther away.

It followed them across the courtyard. It must have been a little drunk: it occasionally staggered. Its stomach rumbled, sounding like the English word "sorry."

The group of pleasure-seekers wandered through the formal gardens. Bushes and trees were cut in the shapes of birds and beasts. The sloppy dragon-head creature left the party guests there and strolled off toward the stables and dog kennels.

"No more champagne for you!" called the party guests as they watched Sloppy Dragon-Head stumble.

It raised one of its four hands.

Clay, in the bottom part of the four-armed coat, was walking as straight as he could. Luckily, Amos was pretty light: he had bird bones. Amos nudged Clay with his heels when he wanted him to turn one direction or the other.

Through the slit in the front of the coat, Clay caught glimpses of the incredible palace of the Kingdom Under the Mountain. He wondered what went on in all those towers and staircases. He wished he could explore the whole thing. But there was no time. Clay decided that somehow, someday, he would come back.

"Stairs. Down," whispered Amos.

Clay slowed up and felt the ground with his toes. There were steps. Carefully, he walked down them, steadying himself on the stone handrail.

The sloppy dragon-head creature was in the stables and kennels. Most of the stables were empty; the court's horses were up above at the festivities. Sloppy Dragon-Head wobbled down the row of gates as Amos looked for the door into the kennels.

There! Barking! Elphinore! The boys could hear her.

A man was yelling at her. Amos was so excited he kicked Clay, trying to steer him to the door.

Down one step, and they were in the dog kennels. Elphinore was cowering in the corner while one of the hound squires screamed in his language, "Into the cage! Go! Bad dog! Bad dog!"

Clay, of course, could not understand the words, but he could tell from the anger and spite in the voice exactly what was being said.

The squire reached for Elphinore. She flinched and tried to flicker away, to appear somewhere else—but just as she started to flicker, the hound squire grabbed her collar. He yanked her toward the cage. A shadow fell across him. He turned to see a weird creature wobbling in the doorway.

"Who are you?" he growled. "Who let you in?"

In a hooty, raspy sort of voice, Sloppy Dragon-Head said, "I visit! See castle."

"Who are you with?" asked the hound squire, looking around for a guide or host.

"With self. Just tall!" Suddenly, Sloppy Dragon-Head lurched to the side and almost fell over. The hound squire looked suspicious. Sloppy Dragon-Head explained apologetically, "First day on Earth." Its upper two hands closed as if in prayer. Its lower two hands wheeled around and looked for something to grab.

By now Elphinore had sat up. She was interested. Her nose twitched. Her eyes blinked rapidly.

"Good dog!" said Sloppy Dragon-Head.

"Bad dog!" said the hound squire. "She went to live with a human-head."

But Elphinore didn't care what anybody said. She could smell the boy. He was right there. She leaped to her feet. Her tail wagged. He was hiding! A game! She pranced toward him.

"Stop!" yelled the hound squire. "Stop! Bad girl!" He raised up his wooden stick to beat her.

Elphinore wriggled to the side, prepared for the blow, but she couldn't contain her excitement. The boy had come for her! The boy was there! She planted her front paws on the odd, towering figure that smelled so much like Clay.

The hound squire swore at her and swung his stick down. Amos screeched and reached out to grab it from the man's hand—and, at the same time, Clay was knocked backward by the dog.

Sloppy Dragon-Head came apart—Clay fell back and Amos toppled forward, swinging the stick, bashing the squire on the head.

The squire collapsed onto the dogs' pillows.

The elf dog frolicked around the two boys, barking with joy, licking at their faces as they squirmed and struggled out of the four-armed silver coat. The dragon mask was ruined. Amos threw it aside and stood.

"Come on!" said Clay. "Back to the staircase! Come on, girl!"

They ran out of the kennel, out of the stables. Elphinore knew they were headed to the upper world. She didn't know about the old staircase in the tower, though—so she was running directly away from it. Away from the boys.

"Elphinore! This way!" Clay bellowed. He stood in the middle of a gravel path through the formal gardens and waved his arms at her. "Elphinore! No! This way!"

She ignored him and barreled off through an arch.

Guards had heard the shouting. They were looking down from the castle walls. A few of them started to clamber down staircases.

Clay ran after Elphinore, furious that she couldn't understand, calling, "Elphinore! No! No! This way! Good girl!"

Amos ran after him, urging him, "Brother Clay! We must turn back! She is leading us into the heart of the castle!"

She ran up steps—she stopped for a second and looked back, to make sure they were following. Just as Clay hoped he could catch up to her, she darted off again.

"Elphinore!" screamed Clay, but she had leaped up the final step, and then she was gone.

CHAPTER NINETEEN

Clay ran as fast as he could after his beloved elf dog.

A guard rattled out in front of Clay, and Clay drew a deep breath. There was no way around the man. He and Amos barreled right into the guard, knocked him over, and kept pounding after Elphinore.

And there she sat, in a kind of golden gondola, waiting patiently for her boy to arrive. It was an odd machine, covered in plaster cupids and wreaths and gilded grapes, with cables that reached all the way up to the ceiling of the cavern.

Amos and Clay stepped onto it, and the machine swayed on its cables.

The guard was clanking after them, yelling orders in his language.

"It goes up!" said Clay. "She was showing us the way to go up!"

"How, Brother Clay?"

Clay saw a lever like a seesaw, some kind of mechanism attached to brass gears. "Here!" he said.

He didn't need to explain any more to Amos. It was clear what they had to do: they each ran to the opposite side of the seesaw lever and started to creak it up and down, up and down.

The gondola lifted off the paving stones, pulled by the cables.

The boys kept pumping the mechanism—and now the palace was falling away beneath them quickly. Satisfied, Elphinore crawled up on a red velvet seat and watched the two kids work.

Halfway to the ceiling, they passed another gondola going down. The elfin passengers, all wearing glittery party clothes and crowns of flowers, gasped and pointed at the boys and the dog and started yelling.

Amos and Clay kept seesawing. They went up and up and up. They were looking out over a whole city now, and an underground lake that stretched off into the darkness. They saw a forest of stone trees on the far shore. Now they were next to the gemstone sun that lit the city.

And then they were inside a tunnel that led to the surface. Their arms ached. They were breathing hard. Even the owl boy's alert eyes looked weary.

But they had made it to the surface. The boys and the dog were inside the hill that was lifted up on pillars. They could see torches and fireflies floating through the woods. They saw the dancers and the party they had left just an hour and a half before. They also saw the guards who stood around the lifted-up hill.

Elphinore leaped right out of the gondola and ran past the guards. She looked back, grinning, to see if her friends were coming along, too. For a second, the guard didn't see anything unusual about an elf-hound bounding past.

Then the two boys charged by. The guard yelled a warning to the others and ran after the fugitive dog.

Clay heard horns blowing. The crowd was startled to see anyone defy the People Under the Mountain. The music stopped. The dancing stopped. Everyone looked on in horror at the two boys and the dog fleeing into the woods with the guards behind them.

"What . . . do we do?" Clay puffed. "Where do we go?"

"I don't know—I don't, Brother Clay. No place is safe."

"My house!"

"They will ride through the walls as if the house had none."

Horn calls were coming from in front of them as well as behind them.

They could not run forward—or backward—or simply stop running. Clay looked around wildly. It seemed hopeless.

And then he had an idea. "This way!" he called out, and Elphinore saw him swerve. She dashed off ahead of him. He and the owl boy tripped and scrambled after her.

"Where are we going?" Amos asked.

Clay did not answer. Behind them ran the guards. And then, in front of the boys, out of the woods streamed the Hunt—all Elphinore's brothers and sisters and the lords and ladies and the Master of the Hunt. They blew their horns again.

Clay held up his arms and screamed in fury.

A few miles away, in the town of Gerenford, in farmhouses and ranch houses, people heard the distant call of the eerie horns near the mountain on Midsummer's Eve, and they shivered. It was almost morning, but they knew those lonely horns meant that someone—some unlucky person—would not see the dawn.

CHAPTER TWENTY

For years after that Midsummer's Eve, the people of the forest would talk about it as one of the most exciting parties ever: that was the year that the human-head boy tried to steal an elf-hound from the People Under the Mountain. None of the other forest-dwellers were very fond of the People Under the Mountain, who were often cold and cruel and even hunted creatures who could speak and argue. So all the beasts who lived in roots and rocks and under ponds were secretly delighted to see Clay and Amos and Elphinore stand up to the chilly, snobbish lords and ladies who lived deep beneath Mount Norumbega.

As the boys and the dog ran before the wild Hunt, all the creatures of the enchanted wood stood back and watched like it was a sport. They did not dare help—though when the kids ran through a crowd of them, all the horned and whiskered guests pretended not to notice, and turned to each other and talked like it was still a normal party. ("Windy sort of evening, isn't it?" "Malvaise, where you been?") The awful Hunt, stampeding to the edge of the crowd, yelled in their language, "Get out of our way! Move!" But no one was in a particular hurry to move until the boys and their dog got away.

"Can I get anyone drinks?" a steeple-capped beast asked the Royal Hunt.

Clay ran as fast as he could. His father had taught him to calculate distances in the woods, and he figured they had a quarter of a mile left before they reached his goal. If they could just make it that far, he had a plan.

Elphinore ran before him, though she didn't really know where to go. Occasionally she would stop and look back, waiting for his orders. Clay was proud of how fast she could run, and even in the midst of panic, he found himself wondering about her miles per hour. But meanwhile he was ready to collapse. He breathed raggedly. His heart was pounding hard.

The Hunt had broken through the ring of party guests and was on their trail again. Clay figured the dogs would surround them first, barking and leaping, and the riders would follow after.

Then Clay and Elphinore and Amos the Owl Boy ran out of the forest and were beside a lake. The moonlight reflected across the water—but the wind was strong now, and the waves sloshed against the grassy shore.

"The wishing lake!" said Amos.

"Exactly," said Clay. "We got to get up to that end, near the apple trees, right?"

Amos immediately knew what Clay meant: It was time to make a wish. Only a wish could save Clay and Elphinore. Clay had to get to that orchard.

But already, the pack of elf-hounds were around them. Elphinore kept running, but the boys were mobbed with dogs who yipped and growled and barked, a hundred sharp fangs and claws—circling them.

Clay looked longingly toward the apple trees at the end of the lake. He would never make it. He would never get to wish that Elphinore would stay with him in the world of mortal people.

Slowly, the riders of the Hunt were stalking out of the woods at the other end of the lake. Their smiles were sneers. They saw the two boys surrounded by the leaping, brutal pack.

"No, come on!" said Clay. "We can do it! We can make it!" He charged toward the apple trees.

Dogs leaped on him. They pulled him down, nipping and scratching. He screamed and swatted at them with his arms, trying to protect his face.

He could see some duke or lord standing over him, peering down from his horse, showing his teeth.

"Please!" Clay said. He didn't know if he was asking for his own life, or just asking that they would let Elphinore stay with him.

He looked across the water and saw Elphinore standing where he should be standing, among the apple trees, staring back at him. If only he had made it that far . . . He could have protected her.

She stood on the bank, looking across the lake at the Master of the Hunt. She trembled. She saw the boy she loved, the boy who had taken her in; he was surrounded by her sisters and brothers and aunts and uncles, who all tore at him, and she couldn't stand the sight.

She wanted nothing more than to be with him, safe, and to never see the People Under the Mountain again.

That was all it took.

The wind blew harder across the wishing lake. Elphinore had a wish—and so did the Master of the Hunt. By the magic of that sacred lake, she got her wish—and the Master of the Hunt lost his.

There was a rumble of thunder in the air, and the sky lit up.

The heads of the Hunt snapped up, as if a voice had called them all at once. They all looked toward the skies. Clay pushed himself up from the ground. He was covered in scratches and ached all over. The dogs had backed away from him. He crawled off to the side, ready to run. His breath came out in gasps.

But the dogs and the cruel hunters did not seem to see him anymore. They all waited, listening to the sky.

And then, almost faster than the eye could see it, there was another flash in the sky, and the Hunt melted. Horses and riders and dogs and whips and spurs—they all collapsed. They sank like the spray of a fountain had shut off. They bled into the ground.

Clay and Amos stared at each other in shock. A wish had been granted, and one had been taken away.

The Hunt was gone. Called down beneath the earth to their kennels and castles. On the shores, the grasses blew in the wind. There was no sign of the People Under the Mountain other than hoofprints in the mud.

And as the dawn broke and Midsummer's Eve ended, Elphinore ran to be at the side of her boy, Clay, and his friend, the owl child—safely and securely forever.

Elphinore licked the boy's face, which was smeared with blood from the dogs' scratching claws. Amos was standing by his side. The grass was trampled down by the horses—but the horses themselves were gone.

"Brother Clay," said Amos, holding out his hand. "Are you well now?"

"Yup," said Clay, and he threw his arm around the dog, who leaped up to put her paws on his chest as he tried to rise.

"Thanks," said Clay.

"You beat the People Under the Mountain," said Amos.

"We did," Clay agreed.

They looked around them. In the branches and leaves of the trees were gathered the guests of Midsummer's Eve, all preparing to go back to their lairs and burrows and secret villages.

The owl-head people, however, stood in lines on the grass. The elders, Brother Mordenai and Sister Hesther, walked toward the boys. They looked fierce, though dressed in starchy antique clothes.

"Clay Human-Head," said Hesther, "you broke our commandment and returned to our dancing hill. The Royal Hunt has already destroyed your home—"

"What?" cried Clay.

"But there is another punishment due to you, so you may

never lead your human-headed kind to our village."

Clay looked to Amos for support—but the owl-head boy was bent down from the waist, as if stuck in the middle of a bow.

Amos said, "I request you do no harm to my friend. He is a good friend, as he showed when he risked his life for this dog beneath the mountain."

The elders did not reply. Hesther said, "Take the dog, Clay Human-Head, and go to that end of the lake, where the Master of the Hunt Under the Mountain lost his wish. Brother Mordenai and I will go this way, to the orchard, and make our wish for Midsummer Morn." She pointed with a scrawny arm at the apple trees where Elphinore had stood and longed for Clay and safety. Hesther said, "We are taking away the dog's ability to walk between worlds. And we are taking away your memory of our village—and all who live within it." With these final words, she glared at Amos, who still stood half-bowing in front of her.

"You can't make me forget Amos!" said Clay. "We're friends!"

Mordenai grabbed Clay by the neck and shoved him toward the end of the lake where a wish would be snatched away.

There was no way out. Clay had broken the rules, and he had to pay the price.

"Say farewell," said Sister Hesther.

The two boys, human-head and owl-head, faced each other. Clay stuck out his hand. The owl boy shook it again, as if they were adults.

"Goodbye, Amos," said Clay. "You've shown me all sorts of amazing things."

"Farewell, Clay Human-Head," said Amos. "I will not forget our adventures."

"The time comes," said Sister Hesther, "when all of us forget the games of our childhood. Go, now."

Clay trudged toward the losing end of the lake. Elphinore walked next to him, unsure why everybody seemed so sad.

Above them, the sky turned red with morning. The wind dropped. The sun was coming up in the east.

Clay looked across the quiet lake at the rows of owl-head people, stiff as figures cut out of paper, dressed in their long coats and wide dresses. And among them was Amos, his friend. His friend forev—

Clay woke up shivering. He was covered with dew. It was Midsummer morning, and he was on the path right behind his house. Elphinore, unconcerned, was digging up a lady slipper.

Rising, seeing the scratches all over his arms and hands, the boy could not remember why he had slept in the woods. Only a dream: the voice of a friend, whispering, "Someday."

Chapter Twenty-One

When Clay and Elphinore got home, everyone was relieved to see them. There were hugs and shouts all round. "Where were you, honey?" his mother sobbed, and he couldn't answer.

"How'd you get all scratched up?" his father demanded, and he didn't know.

"What happened?" asked the police, and he couldn't tell them.

"Great job getting the doggo back," whispered DiRossi. "How's the owl boy?"

"Owl boy?" said Clay, confused.

The O'Brians' house had been destroyed. The windows were broken and everything inside was smashed to pieces. Nobody could say who had done it, though they figured it was the same set of crazy rich horse people who had probably knocked Clay over the head and made him forget everything. The police were looking for the culprits.

They would never find the wrongdoers, and the old-timers in the town of Gerenford knew why.

If there was one good thing that came out of having his house wrecked, it was that Clay's family went to live on his friend Levi's farm for a couple months while they decided what to do next. So after months, Clay and Levi could actually see each other. Clay could show off Elphinore, who loved having two families' worth of kids to play with. She was a big favorite, once people convinced her that the cows were not her enemies.

The kids went swimming with her and played ball and Frisbee with her. She loved to watch them do weird human tasks, like putting up a rope swing and leaping into the river. She hunted the stones at the water's edge for crayfish. She went everywhere with Clay and at night snored gently, resting her head on his arm.

Clay's parents were so worried about what they were going to do about their house that they didn't have time to worry about the global sickness anymore. When they were alone in the bedroom the whole O'Brian family shared, Clay's mom and dad would argue in whispers about money and insurance and all sorts of other things. They had no idea how they were ever going to fix all the damage of Midsummer's Eve.

One day, Clay remembered something. A faint something, because he was kind of confused whenever he tried to think about the woods near Mount Norumbega and the way he'd found his Bulgarian elf-hound.

"Where's Elphinore's old collar?" he asked. "The one she had when I found her?"

"Why?" his mom wondered.

"Because I'm really sure . . ." He tried to think it out, but nothing made sense. He tried again: "I'm really sure that she used to be owned by rich people, and I think the gems all over that collar were probably real."

"That's ridiculous," said Mrs. O'Brian. "They were huge, honey. They wouldn't just be on a dog collar."

Clay shook his head. "Elphinore belonged to someone really rich," he insisted.

Mr. and Mrs. O'Brian looked at each other. They did not look happy. Their mouths were open.

"Yeah!" said DiRossi, suddenly excited. "He's right! Where is it? If those are real, they could solve all our problems!"

Mrs. O'Brian shook her head. She said, "We didn't know. We threw it away, Clay. It's gone. We threw it in the trash weeks ago."

DiRossi burst out, "You're kidding! You did? That is so stupid! I can't believe it!"

Mr. O'Brian firmly told DiRossi to stop talking to her mother that way. Juniper quickly left the room before the yelling started.

Clay, meanwhile, was staring at the ceiling. Something had joggled his memory. He whispered, "The People Under the Mountain." He hadn't been hit over the head by rich, drunk horse people from some resort. He had angered the People Under the Mountain. There had been a palace. How was that possible? It must be a dream. But he remembered it exactly: the towers, and some kind of a machine he had to work with someone else . . . a friend . . . But which friend? It wasn't Levi. It wasn't Wei. It wasn't Paul Versnavsky.

He interrupted his sister, who was being yelled at. He said, "DiRossi, will you tell me what you know about a party in the woods?"

She looked as if she'd been trapped.

Her parents growled, "Yes, DiRossi. *Tell us* about a big party in the woods."

And things might have gotten kind of angry and danger-ous if Juniper hadn't reappeared.

"If you want the diamonds and stuff from Elphinore's collar," she said, "I used them to make my mask sparkle." She held up the cardboard mask. It looked awful: the eyes were holes bashed through with scissors, and the mouth was crooked, and it was covered with glue and sequins. But the nose and the eyebrows and the teeth were all huge, precious gemstones, glittering in the morning light. She said, "I took them off that collar when I saw it in the trash. I wanted to make my mask good."

Her brother and sister and mother and father gaped at her.

"Oh, it's good," her father gasped. "Really, really good, Juniper."

Mrs. O'Brian took the mask and looked at the gems in the light. "Oh," she said. "Oh, yes. I think these are real. They're really real. We didn't even bother to look at them."

"I looked," said Juniper.

"Honey," said her mother, "what if we made another mask together, and took this one apart to save the family?"

"Maybe," said Mr. O'Brian, "we might want to move to a house somewhere else in town—not so close to that forest?"

The forest. Clay wanted to see the forest again. He was starting to remember.

Later that day, he and DiRossi rode their bikes over to their house with Elphinore jogging along behind them. They ditched their bikes in the bushes.

Though they'd only been gone for a couple of days, the house they'd grown up in seemed like someplace they had never been. It already looked like a ruin from long ago. The windows were blank, without a shard of glass in them. Part of the roof was sagging. Was it Clay's imagination, or had all the plants around the house grown taller already? The lawn was as high as meadow grass. There were creepers curling up under the windows. The front door had swung open and orange pine needles were scattered over the floor. Soon, there would be no difference between inside and outside. The two stared at the place they had lived.

"I don't want to move away from the forest," said Clay. "This is where we've always been."

"With those gems," said DiRossi, "Mom and Dad can build a new house anywhere in town. The virus will be over someday. We don't have to be out here in the middle of nowhere."

Clay walked up to the house and pressed his hand against the wall. "I want to keep living here. There's something about those woods. I can't remember . . ."

DiRossi frowned. "Nothing?" she said.

"Nothing of what?" said Clay.

The two started walking along the old path into the woods. Elphinore barreled past them, sailing through the woods in a white streak.

DiRossi began telling Clay what she knew.

There is no way to forget true friendship, because there's too much to remind you of it. DiRossi told him there was a town of owls, and he could picture a boy—no, an owl—yes, an owl boy. The scratches on his arms reminded him of the Hunt, and running from the Hunt, and that reminded him of the friend who had risked his own life to run at his side. DiRossi told him about the blue giant Vud, and he remembered Elphinore waking the giant by barking into its nose. Hazily, he remembered it all, piece by piece, the party and the palace, the stories of all the lost places.

Of course, they could no longer visit any of those places.

Elphinore dashed through the woods, delighted to be back. She balanced her way along old stone walls. She lapped at the streams that gushed down from the mountain. She didn't care much that she couldn't find the places she used to know: frankly, wild turkeys muttering in the woods were much more exciting to her than half-buried blue giants. She was just happy to be out in the sun, running alongside her pack, these human-head people, that brother and sister.

They walked the paths that led up the side of Mount Norumbega. They passed a clock in a tree, but there was no sign of any standing stones or hidden lake. They climbed up the slopes. Aspens and birch trees gave way to dark spruce and sweet-smelling firs. Toward the top of the mountain, the trees were squat and goblinish from all the winds that blew in the winter.

At the top, there was only granite and a few grasses. In all directions was blue distance. DiRossi walked over to the other side of the mountaintop to look toward cities she'd never been to but had always dreamed of visiting, the places she wanted to live when she grew up. Clay sat next to his dog, who was panting happily, and looked down at the forest below them. He saw Owl's Head Hill. There was no village visible there now. He thought about the wishing lake and Amos the owl-head boy. They were somewhere down there, too. He would not forget them. He saw the streams that fell through the deep woods and joined rivers. He saw the rivers go down out of the mountains toward the highways and suburbs of other states.

A boy and his dog sat on a mountaintop, and together, they waited for whatever came next.